THE CHRISTMAS HEART

A FEEL-GOOD HOLIDAY ROMANCE

HELENA HALME

D0452954

NEWHURST PRESS

First published 2018

Paperback ISBN: 978-0-9957495-1-1
Ebook ISBN: 978-1-9998929-9-9

For my long-suffering Englishman

ONE

The lift came to a sudden halt and Tom cursed under his breath. He hated anchor lifts, but the Scandinavians seemed to love them. In the Alps, where he usually skied, they had the good sense to invest in gondolas, in which you could ascend the mountains with some style and no effort. And it was so bloody cold. He'd seen from the large thermometer at the ski hire centre that it was -15C. His carefully groomed stubble was now white and brittle with frost, his lips dry, his cheeks burning from the chill wind cutting into the mountainside. The lift suddenly started again. Slowly, oh so slowly, Tom, perching alone on the two-seater bar, ascended the mountain. He cursed his old friend – why come to a ski resort for the holidays if you want to stay in bed half the day? When Ricky hadn't showed up at breakfast that morning Tom had sent him a WhatsApp. When Ricky replied – 15 minutes later – he said he was having a lie-in and would meet up with Tom later.

Finally, at the top of the small mountain, Tom freed himself from the lift and skied towards the slope. He'd had the foresight to take a piste map from the hotel reception. Åre was different from how it had been in his youth; new slopes had been added and some of the old ones redesigned. He was on his way to one of the few pistes that was served by a proper lift.

There'd been a pretty blonde behind the desk of the hotel and he'd stopped himself from flirting with her just in time. She'd looked barely twenty, and more suitable girlfriend material for his sons than him. Oh, how drab and boring it was to be an old man. He thought about his family, the two boys, Luca and Marco, now 21 and 24, who were in Milan for Christmas with Emma, his ex, and her new husband. He was not welcome at that gathering. Truthfully, he would rather be here with the Nordic winds nearly cutting the nose off his face, and with a potentially embarrassing rendezvous on the horizon, rather than with his loud, disapproving in-laws and the oh-so-wonderful George. He missed his boys, of course, but he'd see them for New Year, when they'd promised to spend a couple of days with him in his new flat in Helsinki.

If only his mother hadn't been taken so suddenly six months ago, he would now be enjoying a luxurious celebration in her central Milan flat. How he missed her!

Oh, well, he thought, as he spotted Father Christmas, his red costume flapping in the wind, zigzagging at speed down the pathetic little mountain – a hill really. He'd go along to the date, have a meal with her, give her a kiss goodnight afterwards and then never see her again.

TWO

The snow hung heavy on the pine trees as Kaisa and Tuuli drove towards Åre, the Swedish ski resort. The Christmas lights from the few houses they passed twinkled over the mounds of snow on either side of the road. The whiteness of the landscape was so intense that it almost blinded Kaisa. They passed a lake, and suddenly a strip of vivid orange appeared above the line of pine trees, the glow of the sun, which had only just set. Kaisa pointed out the vibrant colours to Tuuli, who was driving their hired Volvo.

'This was a good idea, wasn't it?' Tuuli smiled.

'Yes,' Kaisa sighed and closed her eyes.

The morning flights from Helsinki via Stockholm had taken the best part of the day, and she'd not been able to sleep the night before the journey. She was only going to spend a week – the Christmas week – with her best friend in Åre, but during the long hours of the night she'd worried whether she should have stayed with her mother in Helsinki. Jetting off with her friend seemed selfish; she'd heard it in her sister Sirkka's voice on the phone and seen it in her mother's eyes when she'd said goodbye, giving her the presents to put under her small tree in the flat in Helsinki.

But she couldn't bear a traditional Christmas without Rosa. When her daughter, her beautiful 26-year-old daughter, had announced in August that she would go travelling for six months in the autumn, leaving her alone for the holidays, Kaisa had held back the tears that pricked her eyelids. Rosa had been so excited; she'd spent the last two years working hard at an ad agency in central Helsinki, saving her money.

'I'm getting an open return, so I can come home at any time. And,' here she'd hugged Kaisa, placing her arm around her mother's shoulders, reminding Kaisa again that her daughter, now a grown-up, was taller than her. 'We can keep in touch every day. I can Skype you from all the places I've booked ahead.' Rosa's dark green eyes, so clearly her father's, were sparkling. Her auburn hair, cut into a short crop, was ruffled, and Kaisa saw she could hardly contain her elation. She remembered when Rosa was a little girl and would jump up and down with excitement, clapping her hands. Now, she swayed a little instead, moving her lanky body as if to a slow piece of music.

Kaisa smiled; she could never resist Rosa's enthusiasm. Then she remembered something, 'What about your job?'

Rosa went quiet, and looked down at her black Nike trainers.

'I quit.'

'What!'

'Look, mum. I know it's a good job, but they said they'd take me back if there is a position when I return. And I'm sure there will be.'

Kaisa said nothing. Noticing she'd crossed her arms over her chest, she immediately freed her hands. She didn't want to appear confrontational.

'Mum, if I don't travel now when I'm young and not in a relationship, when will I? Just look at Sia! She's been with Jukka since the Lyceum, and there's no way she can go anywhere without him now. All they're thinking about is saving for a place of their own!'

Kaisa had sighed. Rosa was right; her daughter's best friend was on her way to settling down. As comforting as that was for her parents, whom Kaisa knew well, they'd also said they were worried that it was all far too soon. But how could any of them stop 26-year-olds from doing what they wanted? Kaisa herself had already been married to Rosa's father, Peter, her Englishman, at the same age.

Rosa had always been good; she'd never had any problems with her over boys, drugs, drinking or even smoking. Kaisa was sure she'd done some of those things, or even all of them, with Sia, but her daughter had never been in trouble of any sort, or brought trouble home. It was quite remarkable really, having had no father, and having two countries, two languages.

'Besides, mum,' Rosa had added, moving away from her mother and hugging the cup of coffee Kaisa had poured for her before they'd begun this serious discussion. She sat down on a white leather-covered stool. Kaisa had recently replaced the tired-looking high chairs that they'd had at the breakfast bar for twenty-five years – the length of time they'd lived in the two-storey wood-cladded house in Lauttasaari.

'I know you'll be OK with mummu and aunt Sirkka and that lot. But I can't bear the thought of a Christmas without the phone call from Wiltshire.' Rosa spoke into her coffee cup.

Now it was Kaisa's turn to go and put her arms around her daughter.

Peter's parents had passed away in quick succession the previous spring. First it had been his father, who'd had a massive heart attack, and then Viv had just withered away. There had been no evident reason for her death, apart from the fact that her heart had stopped beating. Kaisa knew she had died of a broken heart and sometimes wondered if she would have done the same, if it hadn't been for Rosa, when she lost the love of her life, Peter, twenty-seven years ago.

'OK,' Kaisa had said. 'But you'll have to keep your promise on those daily Skype calls, young lady!'

THREE

Kaisa brushed aside the sinking feeling each time she thought about Rosa and where she might be at that very moment. She'd often wake up in the middle of a preposterous dream of her daughter being held captive somewhere, by men in dirty clothes, their faces half-covered in makeshift masks, or dangling from a branch in a wild forest like Tarzan's Jane, a lion or other wild animal pacing below. Instead of dwelling on all the ills her daughter could fall foul of, Kaisa glanced at her friend's profile. Tuuli had a concentrated look on her face, but when she sensed her friend's gaze, she turned and smiled.

Kaisa thought that a Christmas holiday away from it all was perfect for her friend too. It was Tuuli's second Christmas without her mother, but more importantly, she'd managed to settle her elderly father into a sheltered apartment in a retirement home this autumn. Her dad had been adamant that Tuuli should go and enjoy herself rather than, as her father had put it, 'Spend the holidays with the soon-to-be-departed.' Tuuli's dad was a retired teacher, and he'd never been demanding of Tuuli's time. Kaisa smiled. It was from her father that Tuuli had inherited her no-nonsense approach to life, the attribute that had often lifted Kaisa out of the mire of grief over Peter, and helped her overcome the struggles to raise a child on her own. Now that same quality had brought her here to the beautiful Scandinavian mountain range.

'Tired?' Tuuli said, jolting Kaisa away from her thoughts. They'd arrived in Åre, where the friends had first skied in the early days of Kaisa's return to Finland. This was their third time skiing here, but they'd never stayed in such an expensive place before. They'd agreed that for a Christmas holiday they'd pull out all the stops. They'd decided on Tottbacken, a three-storey building with views across Lake Åre and the ski village below. It advertised itself as one of the best places to stay in Åre. It was a ski-in, ski-out lodge, next to an anchor lift that took you up the mountain. Following the instructions emailed to them, Tuuli drove up the hill away from the main road that ran alongside the lake. They turned onto a smaller private road, which snaked further up the hill. Leaving behind the houses clad in dark wood, their balconies and windows strung with Christmas lights, they eventually parked in front of a large house built into the snowy mountain. It had two Alpine-style sloped roofs, with four large balconies.

Kaisa glanced at her friend and smiled, 'It's beautiful.'

Large Christmas stars adorned the windows, and there was a layer of snow on the roofs as well as the low-slung stone structure that served as a car port below.

'We have the middle floor to the left,' Tuuli said. 'And I believe we can park inside.'

Kaisa glanced at the temperature gauge in the car; it showed -17C.

'But we have to wait for someone to come and open up.'

There was a slight snowfall, which gave the whole scene a magical air. The two women grabbed their warm padded coats from the back seat and got out of the car. Behind them, the Christmas lights of the ski village shimmered in the late afternoon dimness. The sun, which had set at the bottom of the valley beyond Lake Åre an hour or so earlier, had left a faint peachy light along a layer of cloud. Gone were the flaming colours they'd witnessed during the drive. They stood for a while admiring the view. Kaisa's friend took a deep breath and gazed at the fairytale scene in front of her.

'It's going to be a perfect day for skiing tomorrow!'

What a contrast, this silence, the pure air, and the lights reflecting in the snow was to the dark and miserable Helsinki they'd left behind that morning. In the capital, they'd had only one snowfall that autumn, early in October. Then the snow had come in a storm, some 15 centimetres falling overnight, but by the following day all the snow had melted, leaving just a scattering of dirty-looking patches here and there at the side of the roads. In Lauttasaari, where Kaisa lived overlooking the sea, the snow had stayed a day or so longer than in the centre of the city, but even there by December, the constant rain and sleet made the landscape look dark and bleak. Everyone in Finland was obsessed about having a white Christmas, but not in Helsinki, not this year.

Kaisa breathed in the clean air and gave her friend a hug. 'Thank you for convincing me this was a good idea!'

Before Tuuli had time to reply, a thin blonde woman emerged from the building wearing a wide smile. 'Welcome to Tottbacken!' she said and opened the door to the large garage housed at the entrance of the building.

The apartment the young woman showed the friends was more luxurious than any ski chalet, or hotel, Kaisa had ever seen. The beds looked wide and blissfully comfortable, the linen was pure Egyptian cotton, and a new sauna was attached to a double walk-in shower. They each had their own bathroom and views over the village in the valley and across Lake Åre. In the living area, there was even a small Christmas tree, adorned with stylish ski-themed decorations.

FOUR

The next morning, after a deliciously long lie-in, Kaisa and Tuuli put on their snow suits, slung their skis over their shoulders, and made their way to the ski lift, just behind the chalet. Kaisa felt a little shaky on her skis. It had been ten months since she'd last been on the slopes. They had to make their way up the snowy edge of the piste, where the snowploughs had deposited the excess snow, and then ski down a short part of the slope towards the lifts. Kaisa was relieved when she pulled up next to Tuuli. As they waited in the queue, Kaisa glanced up the length of the piste. She noticed that just by the entrance to the ski store of their apartment, where they'd come from, there was a patch of ice. The slight wind had removed the thin layer of snow that had covered it. She made a mental note to avoid that spot when they returned at the end of the day.

As Tuuli had predicted, it was perfect skiing weather; although it was cold, faint sunlight illuminated the mountaintop. The pistes were well prepared; the stripey pattern created by the snow-ploughs was broken only in the very middle of the slope, where the few skiers were swishing down the mountainside. The scenery at the top looked inviting.

The slopes were not as busy as either of them had expected. Tuuli, who had spent several Christmas holidays in Sweden, had warned Kaisa that they may not be able to go skiing as often as they would like; it could be stormy, too cold or too windy.

'And when the weather is good, everyone will be on the pistes,' she'd warned Kaisa.

But today, everything was perfect. There were other skiers about, but they didn't disturb their day. Even the sun peeked out from behind the clouds for an hour or so, making the snow sparkle under its rays.

At one point they'd passed two guys dressed in Father Christmas outfits. They'd waved and wished *God Jul* to the two women. Their skiing was erratic and dangerous-looking, so Kaisa and Tuuli stopped on the side of the piste and watched them make their way down the mountain.

'They've had a few too many *glöggs*, I think!' Tuuli laughed.

'The last Christmas' by Wham was blaring out of the speakers as their lift deposited them on top of the mountain furthest from Tottbacken. Kaisa suddenly had the most overwhelming Christmas feeling. Peter had loved this song, and usually she'd feel tearful just hearing it. But not today, not looking at the view in front of her, of almost deserted pistes above snow-capped pine trees with a bluish sky and opaque sun.

After two hours of energetic skiing, Tuuli suggested they stop at one of the bars on the mountainside for a *glögg*. They were close to a restaurant called Fjällgården. She chin pointed down the hill. 'You ready?'

Kaisa nodded and followed Tuuli down towards a snow-capped building clad in dark wood at the bottom of the piste. Kaisa enjoyed the mountain views almost as much as the thrill of moving fast down the piste, controlling the turns while letting the skis take her freely down. Half-way down she noticed a Christmas tree twinkling outside the restaurant and people milling about the entrance.

Fjällgården was a pretty Alpine-style restaurant,

buzzing with skiers. Inside, the lights were low, barely showing off the high wooden ceiling and huge chandeliers made out of reindeer antlers. There was a bar with a few long tables in the middle, with benches on either side, filled with youngsters drinking and laughing. Tuuli moved further back into the large restaurant beyond, where they found two free sofas opposite a huge open fire in the middle of the room.

'This is excellent,' Tuuli said, removing her helmet and settling herself opposite Kaisa. They lifted the glasses of hot *glögg* they'd ordered.

'Here's to a wonderful holiday!' Tuuli said.

The scented wine warmed Kaisa's body. She glanced at her phone and saw it was nearly three o'clock. She also saw she'd had a missed Skype call from Rosa and immediately dialled her number.

'Sorry mum, can't talk now. I'm OK, it's really hot here and all is well. Byeee.'

'Bye, love you,' Kaisa replied and then the line went dead.

'Your goddaughter is alive and well anyway,' she said to Tuuli, and they clinked their glasses again.

'That's good to hear,' Tuuli said and finished her drink. 'Another?'

Kaisa looked at her friend. 'We're not skiing any more then?'

'No, don't think so, do you? The lifts close in half an hour, but we can take the little train from here to Tott Hotel, which is just by our apartment. I'm having a beer. I think I've earned it, you?'

Sometimes Kaisa wondered where Tuuli put all the food and drink she consumed. She was still as slim as she'd been when they'd been students together at Hanken, the Swedish-language school of economics Kaisa had remarkably gained entry to after her Baccalaureate exams. Tuuli had a job where she mostly sat down all day, but she did do a lot of sport – skiing in winter and golf in the summer. Kaisa too had taken up both sports, but she was much less committed and had put on a few extra kilos in her fifties. Now at fifty-seven, she was constantly fighting the bulge. She couldn't honestly call herself fat, but she was almost a size larger than she had been in her twenties. Some people, like her sister, said the few extra pounds suited her, making Kaisa look 'less angular', but she knew Sirkka and the others were just being kind.

Kaisa made a promise to herself to start 2018 with a new exercise regime, increasing the number of times a week she went swimming in the old Yrjönkatu baths in Helsinki. She had no excuse not to go, because the swimming pool was close to where she worked as a freelance translator and English teacher. She didn't need to work – Peter, the husband she lost when she was just thirty years old, had seen to it that her finances were better than good – but she couldn't stay at home, and she needed the social interaction a job afforded.

When she'd first come over to Helsinki in the early 1990s, she'd worked for YLE, the Finnish equivalent of the BBC. She'd been a journalist on a half-day basis, and had put Rosa into the local English nursery. That had worked well until there were some changes at the corporation, and Kaisa had found the politics too much. She'd applied for redundancy in 2010 and had begun translating and teaching for a local Finnish/British charity. She enjoyed the interaction and social engagements that the charity arranged with Brits in the city, and liked teaching youngsters and adults English.

FIVE

At the end of what had turned out to be a good day's skiing, Ricky suggested they have a beer or two in the hotel bar. He had finally joined Tom at the Olympia lift around 12 noon, after he had skied down the Western side of Åreskutan, his favourite part of the resort, twice.

'It's the spot for après-ski, nowadays,' he said and smirked at Tom.

As Tom entered the rowdy bar, he was reminded of their younger days when he, Ricky and the other boys from their university used to spend at least a week on the slopes during the winter holidays. He dreaded to think how close he'd been to breaking a leg or having some other kind of accident during those weeks. As well as skiing, there'd been a lot of drinking, late nights in bars at the top of the mountain followed by skiing down the slopes in darkness – full of beer and often vodka chasers too. He remembered that he'd once brought a girl down who couldn't ski. The girl in reception that morning had reminded him of her, he now realised. She had also had blonde hair, with alabaster skin, and the same pale blue eyes. The girl from years ago had a slight build, so he'd placed her skis between his, and they'd snowploughed down the mountain in a straight line. He couldn't even remember her name now, but he still recalled that she'd screamed the whole way down. He shook his head and smiled.

'What's funny?' Ricky asked. He was momentarily stopped by a young kid carrying a tray full of beer glasses. They'd been pushing through a throng of youngsters. Now Tom's friend looked at him questioningly.

'Nothing, I just remembered something.' Tom stopped dead. The waiter had disappeared into a door to the side and there was a clear view of a set of sofas facing a fireplace that separated the rowdy bar from the hotel restaurant. On the sofa sat two women in ski-gear whom Tom recognised. He grabbed Ricky's arm and turned abruptly around.

'You said we'd meet them tomorrow night!'

Ricky gave him a startled look. His wild demeanour was highlighted by his hair, which was pointing in all directions now that he'd taken his ski helmet and balaclava off. Instinctively, Tom went to touch his own head, brushing his hair down with his fingers.

'Look, I'm not ...' Tom was struggling to say what he meant. 'I thought it was going to be just you and me tonight.'

Ricky let out a small laugh. He was looking sheepishly at his friend.

'Ah, I was going to mention that. It's fine, they're really good fun,' Ricky said. His eyes were downcast, suddenly intrigued by the workings of the clasp of his helmet.

Tom was staring at his friend in disbelief.

Ricky lifted his eyes to Tom.

'C'mon, they won't bite. Let's get a couple of beers first,' he said, touching Tom's arm.

Tom said nothing but followed his friend to the bar, glancing briefly at the two women. He'd seen Tuuli quite a few times since Ricky had started seeing her, and was once again taken aback by how little she had changed since their university days. In her a tight-fitting cream polo neck under the wide straps of her ski trousers, he saw clearly the outline of those large breasts that had got many a guy's head spinning in Hanken, although he'd never been attracted to Tuuli himself. Probably because he'd preferred her friend.

Tuuli was leaning back on the sofa, saying something to Kaisa, who had her back to Tom. All he could see of Kaisa was her profile and her slender shoulders covered by a pink top. Her hair was blonde, as before, and she also looked slim and younger than she was. He'd turned sixty the year before so Kaisa must be around fifty-five, perhaps a few years older? She seemed to be laughing at something Tuuli had said, the way she dipped her head and moved her shoulders up and down. Suddenly, Kaisa turned and looked in the direction of the bar. Quickly, Tom swung his face away. Luckily the place was dimly lit, and with the fire illuminating the two women, he hoped Kaisa wouldn't have spotted him observing her from a distance.

Tom suddenly felt a tingle of excitement at the prospect of seeing Kaisa again. The fear and resentment he'd felt about the prearranged date was quickly fading. Perhaps it was a good idea to make friends with Kaisa at last, to wipe away their previous encounters? Or even something more?

SIX

'Look who I found skulking around the bar!' Tuuli said. She was holding two beers and behind her Kaisa saw two taller shapes.

When one of them came into the light she saw it was Ricky, Tuuli's partner. Kaisa was puzzled when Ricky stepped forward to give her a hug. Tuuli hadn't mentioned that Ricky would be in Åre for Christmas. In fact, she was almost sure her friend had told her that he had to be with his elderly parents for the holidays. Ricky was wearing a bright red ski suit, tight around his narrow hips. He moved slowly forward, hampered by his ski boots. It was only when Kaisa looked over Ricky's shoulder, still in his friendly, but tight embrace, that she saw him. Her breath caught in her throat and she pulled herself away from Ricky.

Tom came forward and offered Kaisa his hand.

'Hi, it's been a long time,' Tom said and grinned like a naughty schoolboy.

Kaisa took the proffered hand and felt his strong fingers around her own. Their eyes met. Kaisa's mind returned to the first time she'd ever seen him, in the Hanken Students' Union bar where he had so obviously hit on her, giving her the once-over, his eyes lingering on Kaisa's hips, breasts and lips for far too long. And then the meeting a couple of years later, when Kaisa had fled Scotland – and the wrongs she had done to Peter – to sleep on her sister's sofa bed in Helsinki. She'd thought that her marriage to Peter was over and she needed to move on. Tom and Kaisa had a date but it had gone disastrously wrong. Since that evening, Kaisa hadn't set eyes on one of the 'Rich Boys', as she and Tuuli had dubbed the gang of wealthy students.

'Yes,' she eventually managed to stutter.

Kaisa regarded the mature man in front of her. Tom's tidy grey beard (it was just a five-clock shadow, really) was almost white with the frost on it. It looked as if he'd just stepped inside the restaurant. He too was wearing an all-in-one snowsuit, but his was light grey with red stripes on the sides. His dark brown hair looked a little silvery around the temples, but he had the same floppy fringe that he'd always worn.

'Well, isn't this like old times!' Tuuli said, the tone of her voice a little too high, and she asked the two men to join them on the sofas. Kaisa seated herself down quickly, trying at the same time to catch Tuuli's eye. It was obvious her friend had set her up. But Kaisa's friend was chatting to Ricky, who'd sat down next to Tuuli on the seats opposite. With their heads close to each other, they laughed. It was so dark in the restaurant, that Kaisa couldn't see Tuuli's eyes, or rather, the expression in them.

'Can I sit here?' Tom was still standing, with the beer in his hand.

'Ah, sorry, of course,' Kaisa said, moving to the end of the sofa, avoiding those eyes. She turned towards her friend, then looked sideways at Tom, who had settled next to her. She pulled her lips into a smile.

'It must be, what thirty years since ...' Kaisa stammered.

Why did she always have to be so awkward in social situations? Even now when she was in her fifties!

She swallowed hard and continued, '... since I last saw you. What have you been up to?'

Tom coughed into his hand and smiled. Kaisa

noticed how white his teeth were. Even in the low light of the restaurant, Kaisa could tell the man was tanned. Tanned in that central European way that no Finn ever managed, however much tanning lotion they applied. He had a few lines around his eyes and mouth, but they just made him look more attractive. Kaisa wondered about her own appearance. Her hair was probably plastered onto her skull, the result of wearing a ski helmet all day.

'I've been out of the country. Living in Milan. You remember my mother was Italian?' Tom said. He took a swig from his glass.

'Yes, I do.'

Tom was quiet now, looking into his drink and Kaisa didn't know what to say. She leaned towards the table to pick up her beer and to catch Tuuli's eye. She raised her eyebrows and hoped her friend would come to her aid. But Tuuli simply gave a quick smile, and continued to chat to Ricky, unaware (on purpose?) of Kaisa's predicament.

'Sorry, I had no idea about this,' Kaisa nodded towards her friend and Ricky.

Tom's eyes peered at her with such an intense gaze that she suddenly felt breathless.

'It was rather sprung on me, too,' he laughed.

'Ah,' Kaisa said. She took another, larger gulp of her drink and licked the beer foam off her lips.

'I'm sorry,' Kaisa said.

Tom's eyes widened, 'No need, it's nice to catch up, yes?'

Kaisa nodded, but didn't know what to say.

'As old friends,' Tom said and lifted his pint towards Kaisa.

'Old friends!' Kaisa said and they clinked their glasses.

As he drank his beer, Tom's eyes didn't leave Kaisa's. He kept them there for such a long time that Kaisa eventually had to move her face away. Her mouth felt dry and she realised she was nervous. Or not exactly nervous, but suddenly she could feel Tom's presence acutely. The heaviness of his body on the sofa next to her, their knees nearly touching. Kaisa took another gulp of beer as ladylike as she could muster. If only she'd asked for wine! She didn't like drinking beer, but it seemed appropriate after a day on the slopes. Suddenly she realised this was a neutral subject she could talk to Tom about.

'So, you two are skiing here for the holidays?'

Tom smiled, and there was a glint in his eyes that Kaisa remembered from Hanken. 'It seems so!' Tom gestured at his outfit.

Kaisa laughed, 'Likewise.' She too indicated her ski pants and boots, which she'd unbuckled for comfort.

There was another silence. Kaisa wracked her brain for something else to say. Desperately, she looked over to Tuuli and Ricky, who were just getting up.

'Another round?' she asked Kaisa. 'The boys are paying!' Without waiting for a reply from her friend, Tuuli disappeared to the bar with Ricky. The two clattered away on the stone floor with their boots, leaving the silence between Kaisa and Tom to grow. Eventually she remembered she could ask Tom more about the day's skiing.

'Where did you ...'

'What are you ...' Tom said at the very same time and they both laughed.

Tom leaned closer to Kaisa and put his hand on her thigh. 'It's very nice to see you.'

His touch burned Kaisa's leg, even through the padding on her salopettes. She lifted her eyes up to Tom again and smiled, 'You too.'

SEVEN

'So, are we all looking forward to our Christmas Eve meal at Buustamons?' Tuuli said. Her eyes were bright and Kaisa couldn't help but return her smile. She listened when her friend described the small restaurant on the Western outskirts of the ski resort, where they would serve local food as well as traditional Swedish Christmas goodies.

'Have you been to Åre before?' Tom said quietly, addressing Kaisa after Tuuli had finished. His dark eyes bore into hers and again, Kaisa felt a tingle on her skin, and a warmth flow through her body under his intense gaze.

What are you; a teenage girl?

'Long time ago,' she replied and looked down at her drink.

'I used to come up here a lot during our Hanken time,' Tom said and smiled. 'You know, this was the playground of the 'Rich Boys'. '

Kaisa looked into his eyes and laughed. That was the nickname Tuuli and Kaisa had given the group of wealthy Swedish-speaking students with a reputation for heavy partying and womanising at Hanken. Kaisa had forgotten that she'd told Tom the pet name during their disastrous date some thirty years before. Kaisa wondered how he remembered such a little detail after so much time had passed.

Tom's smile widened and he turned to Ricky. 'Did you know that's what these two ladies used to call us?'

'Is that true?' Ricky said and turned to Tuuli, who'd widened her eyes at Kaisa. But she smiled when she replied, 'I couldn't possibly remember that far back!'

They all laughed and chatted for a while about their university days, about friends they had in common and what they were doing now. Tom said he often thought how little they'd appreciated being young.

'You guys made a good attempt at enjoying life as far as I can remember,' Kaisa said and raised an eyebrow at Ricky.

The two men protested, saying they weren't as bad

as their reputations. Kaisa didn't want to ask how long they'd taken over their degrees. Kaisa knew they'd been studying for their four-year MA for two years by the time Kaisa and Tuuli entered the School of Economics, and they were still apparently studying when she and Tuuli were taking their finals. The 'Rich Boys' seemed to have just one goal in Hanken: party as hard as they possibly could. She wasn't even sure if Tom had graduated in the end. Looking at the man she'd been a little infatuated with at university, the skin around his dark eyes now gaining deep but attractive lines when he smiled, she wondered which one of them had the right idea; perhaps Tuuli and Kaisa had been too serious and goal-driven in those days? Perhaps they would have been better off enjoying life a little more? Although, Kaisa guessed, she'd been more concerned about doing well in her exams so that she could land a good job when she moved to Britain to be with Peter. She hadn't exactly been ambitious just for the sake of her career. Her biggest motivation had been love.

'Oh my, is that the time,' Tuuli suddenly exclaimed.

All the others looked at her. Smiling, she said to Kaisa, 'I've organised a surprise for you!'

Another one, Kaisa thought but said nothing.

'We have to go,' Tuuli said.

Tom stood up, facing Kaisa.

'I'll see you tomorrow then,' Tom said.

'Yes,' Kaisa replied.

Tom leaned towards Kaisa, but she took a step back and he quickly straightened up.

'We'll see you boys tomorrow night. Be good now,' Tuuli said and kissed Ricky on the lips and Tom on his cheek while Kaisa watched.

'Come on,' Tuuli said and took hold of Kaisa's arm.

She waved to both Ricky and Tom and followed Tuuli out of the bar and onto the train that would take them down towards their lodgings. As they walked past Tott Hotel, the old guest house perched just below their apartment building on Tottbacken, Tuuli ducked inside, pulling Kaisa with her and nearly knocking her skis off her shoulders with the movement.

'We've got an appointment here!' Tuuli said and grinned.

Soon the two friends were reclining on lounge chairs, wrapped in white dressing gowns, in a warm room, with aromatherapy candles burning around them, creating a light and calming scent. What Rosa called 'blinkety blink music' played quietly, adding to the serene atmosphere of the space.

'You don't mind the boys being here, do you?' Tuuli said and she sipped some cucumber water given to them by the woman who'd shown them into the room.

She didn't have time to reply before a young man wearing white cotton slacks and a tunic appeared from the narrow corridor.

'Kaisa,' he said, his eyes looking down at a clipboard. When he lifted them, Kaisa noticed how beautiful his chiselled features were.

Kaisa turned to her friend and squeezed her arm, 'We'll talk later.'

She followed the man into a small room.

Inside, more candles surrounded a massage table covered in white fluffy towels.

'Is this your first time?' the man asked. His direct gaze took Kaisa by surprise, but she felt herself falling into the man's bright blue eyes.

Moving her face downwards, Kaisa told the man – or boy – who introduced himself as Niklas, that she'd had many massages before.

'That's good,' Niklas said and added, 'take as much off as you feel comfortable with, lie face down, and cover yourself with the towel. Preferably, you should be naked for me to massage your neck and thighs properly.' He stepped out of the room.

Kaisa wondered if she should mention that, although she'd had many massages before, she'd never been massaged by a man, let alone such a good-looking one. She wondered if she was being oversensitive – even a little English – for feeling an awkward anticipation about being touched by this Niklas.

Yet the man seemed very businesslike when he walked back in and asked what kind of pressure she would like. Lying face down on the table, all Kaisa could see from the small hole where her face was resting, was the man's bare ankles between his white slacks and black leather clogs. He had dark hairs growing on the bridge of his feet. *I'm the problem here, not him,* she thought and closed her eyes.

'Medium,' Kaisa replied and tried to relax into the treatment.

The massage was excellent. Initially, Kaisa was aware of each touch of the young, male masseur, but after a few moments, she forgot where she was and and began to enjoy the tightness around her back, legs and neck loosen. Although his touch was sensitive, and felt sensual to Kaisa, she reminded herself that it was probably just her hormones. Meeting Tom again must be playing tricks on her mind, she thought. She reminded herself that this Niklas was

a. Paid to massage her

and

b. Probably the same age as her daughter.

When Niklas told her to turn around, she felt self-conscious again, even though she saw he had lifted the towel up against himself and was pointedly looking the other way when Kaisa flipped onto her back.

'You are in very good shape. You must exercise a lot?' Niklas, said, once he had replaced the towel and started to massage her left calf.

'Sorry, what did you say?' she said, lifting her eyes to the masseur.

'I'm sorry, that was very unprofessional of me.'

The rest of the time, Niklas worked in silence, only once or twice asking if the pressure he was applying was OK. Kaisa nodded and kept her eyes shut so that she wouldn't betray how good his touch on her body felt. After the comment on her fitness, Kaisa wondered whether the man had been coming onto her after all.

She nodded to him, indicating that all was well, and tried not to enjoy the man's touch too much. But it was useless. Niklas really had a talent for making Kaisa relax. When, finally, he moved his fingers up and down her neck, massaging the top of her spine, Kaisa let out a soft moan.

'That's good, is it?' Niklas said. Kaisa could hear the smile in his words.

'Yes, thank you,' Kaisa said as prudishly as she could, keeping her eyes resolutely shut.

When Niklas told her he was done, Kaisa smiled.

'You are very good,' she said, trying to sound more motherly than sexy. It was true, her muscles felt like new. She was also a little relieved that it was over, until Niklas said, looking down at Kaisa, with his eyes fixed onto hers, 'Is there anything else I can do for you?'

'He really said, "Is there anything else I can do for you?" ' Tuuli exclaimed when they were sitting in the sauna later.

Kaisa nodded. 'I kept thinking there was nothing to it, and that it was all in my imagination, but when, after the comment about me being in good shape, he said that, I knew it wasn't quite innocent after all.'

Tuuli threw some more water onto the hot stones and laughed, 'I just can't believe it!'

'I know!' Kaisa said.

'And I had a boring old woman,' Tuuli said between breaths. The water she'd thrown had produced a stinging wave of heat and both women were doubled over on the wooden benches of the small sauna.

When the heat had abated a little, Tuuli straightened her back and looked at Kaisa with a serious expression. 'Do you think we should report him?'

Kaisa lifted her eyes towards her friend. 'This is what I've been wondering. The thing is, he didn't *do* anything. Apart from give me the best massage ever.'

Tuuli nudged Kaisa's side, grinning, 'You sure that's all he gave you?'

Instead of talking about her massage, Kaisa had wanted to talk to Tuuli about the boys' sudden appearance earlier, but by now she'd lost all her bluster. She even had to admit to Tuuli that she'd enjoyed the men's company, or more precisely Tom's company, when Tuuli came clean and told Kaisa she'd known about Ricky's plans for a couple of weeks.

'He was a bit at a loss this Christmas. His awful wife won't let him see his boys, and Tom didn't want to spend the holidays with his ex-wife and his parents-in-law (who hate Tom). And because Tom's mother passed away not long ago, Ricky decided to invite him to Åre.'

'Oh, I didn't know he lost his mother?' Kaisa said.

Tuuli nodded.

They were both gazing out of the window, which afforded a view down the valley and the village. It was now completely dark, but the many Christmas lights reflecting on the snow made the scene glow with an enchanting shimmer.

'It looks like one of those snow globes, doesn't it?' Kaisa said to her friend.

Tuuli smiled, 'It's going to be a wonderful holiday!'

Kaisa looked at her friend's profile.

'But they're not staying with us?' The apartment in the villa had three bedrooms, one with its own en-suite bathroom and two sharing a large shower room with two sinks and a WC.

Tuuli gave Kaisa a long look. Her bright blue eyes met Kaisa's. 'I didn't know how you'd take it.'

'You could have asked me.'

Tuuli laughed, 'Now, that wouldn't be any fun, now would it?' She added, 'Besides, I wanted you all to myself.'

Kaisa knew Tuuli suspected that she would have said no to the plan, and now thinking about it, Kaisa was sure she wouldn't have agreed. She might even have been a bit upset; their unique Christmas together in the ski resort would have turned into something completely different. Now, however, Kaisa found herself not minding the arrangement at all.

Her friend explained that the two were happy to stay in the smart Fjällgården hotel by the hillside where they'd met.

'You know what Ricky and I are like, we're happier when we're not living together.'

Kaisa nodded, although she really didn't under-stand. After all the years that she'd known Tuuli, some part of her was still a complete mystery to Kaisa. As slim, tall and good-looking as her friend was, she wondered whether Tuuli sometimes felt lonely. Yet she hadn't seen any evidence of this; Tuuli was as even-tempered and mysterious as ever.

She had to admit that Tuuli and Ricky had an unusual relationship. As far as Kaisa could under-stand, they were officially a couple, had been for the best part of thirty years. Yet they had never married, had no children and had never even shared a home together. Nonetheless, it seemed to work for them; both looked happy and were always laughing into each other's eyes. Ricky and Tuuli both now lived in Ullanlinna, only a street away from each other. They went on holidays together and were very much the married couple, but without the conventional para-phernalia. Ricky lavished Tuuli with gifts. He worked in high tech exports and was always travelling, bringing Tuuli the most amazing jewellery and designer handbags and shoes. Kaisa sometimes wondered if it was a guilty conscience that made Ricky spend the astronomical sums that a Louis Vuitton suitcase, or a white gold diamond ring, would set him back, but she didn't even want to broach the subject with her friend. Tuuli was very happy with the arrangement, she knew that much.

'We have the perfect relationship,' she once told Kaisa when they'd had a few too many glasses of champagne. 'If either of us wants to go with someone else, we can. How would a ring and a ceremony change that? If you don't want to be in a relationship, you leave, whatever your legal status, don't you?'

That night in bed, Kaisa couldn't stop thinking about Tom and his eyes upon her. She imagined his slender fingers that had touched her thigh on her neck and running down her bare back, on her breasts, on the inside of her thighs. There was a heat in her body and a desire she hadn't felt for a long time. The massage had revived something in her. Damn that Niklas! But why Tom of all people? Their history wasn't good; besides what did she know about him? For want of another word, he'd been a bit of a

Casanova at university. A player. What was he like now? He had the same build, he'd hardly put on any weight around his middle, unlike most men did in their fifties. Oh, wait, he must be sixty already? An old Lothario! Kaisa smiled to herself in the dark. All that she'd seen and remembered about the man made him more attractive. He was exciting, dangerous, even. Anyway, what was the harm in having a little flirtation over Christmas?

None, she thought, had it not been for the disastrous date they'd had in Helsinki in the late 1980s. If that had shown anything, it had revealed the lack of desire Tom had for Kaisa. No, it was pointless and stupid to think that Tom was after her. He was probably just being polite and Kaisa had completely misread the signals.

As she turned over in bed for the umpteenth time, waiting for sleep to come, she knew his gaze had meant something. He had definitely come onto her. She couldn't be that wrong, could she? As she began to feel drowsy, she remembered what his lips tasted like, and how it would feel to have those strong arms around her. Kaisa fell sound asleep, only to dream that Tom was lying next to her, his legs and arms spooning her.

EIGHT

In the winter, the Buustamons mountain restaurant was inaccessible by car. Tuuli and Kaisa would have to take a taxi to the end of the road, where they'd be met by an old army truck, kitted out with snow chains. It was dark when the two women stepped inside the vehicle, where four other people were already waiting, huddled together in the cold.

Kaisa nodded to the couple who sat nearest to her. '*God Jul!*,' she said, but the woman looked at her incomprehensibly. Kaisa smiled and tried in English, 'Merry Christmas!'

The woman, who was quite young, with very dark eyes and curly hair, which poked out of her pink bobble hat, smiled and said, in an English accent, 'Thank you and Happy Christmas to you too!'

Her voice was enthusiastic and she smiled at Kaisa.

Her partner, a tall man who was sitting hunched up on the bench next to the woman, also wished Kaisa season's greetings.

Kaisa thanked them both, and then turned away from the couple. Knowing how the English were, Kaisa understood the polite thing would have been to ask them where they were from, how they liked skiing in Sweden, and make other such small talk. But she didn't have the energy tonight. Tuuli and Kaisa had been on the mountain all day, and she was physically tired.

The Christmas Eve weather had been glorious on the slopes. The sun was out for nearly the whole day as Kaisa and Tuuli skied down piste after piste. Tuuli, as always on the skiing holidays the women had taken together over the years, had a plan already in place before they even took the first lift up to the top of the mountain. They criss-crossed the terrain, had lunch at the topmost restaurant, and at the end of the day's skiing, stopped for *glögg* at a ski hut close to the piste next to their chalet.

As well as being tired from the day's skiing, Kaisa was also apprehensive about the evening ahead. Her thoughts were on the prospect of spending the evening with Ricky and Tom. She tried not to think about how she felt about Tom, how he'd sneaked into her dreams the night before, how she'd woken up to the memory of the disastrous evening. And how it had ended.

Lying in her bed, listening for any sign that Tuuli was awake, she'd decided that she needed to stop acting like a lovesick puppy around Tom. It was evident from their previous encounter that he didn't have those sorts of feelings for her. And just as well he didn't. The thought of what might have happened if they'd actually made love on that date thirty years before, sent shivers down Kaisa's spine. If it had all gone well and they'd started dating, Kaisa might never have returned to England and reunited with her true love, Peter. She'd never had been given the gift of Rosa, Peter's flesh and blood, who looked so much like him. Yet, was Kaisa wrong in what she'd seen in Tom's eyes when he'd bent his head so close to her the evening before? Was she wrong to think he might have kissed her had they not been sitting on the sofa opposite Ricky and Tuuli? Could she be so bad at reading other people – at understanding men?

Kaisa hadn't had many relationships, that was true. And her one serious relationship had been tumultuous to say the least, even though they had been so happy. Since Peter's tragic death, and her move to Finland, Kaisa had been alone for long periods. Having a small daughter to look after had made ignoring the need for a man easy; she'd decided she didn't want anyone else to bring Rosa up. Instead, she welcomed frequent visits by her two best friends in England, Ravi and Rose. Ravi had eventually become openly gay and found his true love in a tall, handsome architect. He was Rosa's favourite uncle, whereas Rose, a journalist and older friend, brought along her son, until he became too old to tag along to a strange Nordic country with his mother. Joshua, who was two years younger than Kaisa's Rosa, was now at university in Leeds, studying English.

'A chip off the old block,' Rose told Kaisa over the phone just before Christmas. Rose, who'd been responsible for Kaisa's career in journalism, having given her a job on a magazine she edited, still visited Kaisa twice a year, and the two friends spoke on the phone at least once every week. One of the recurring subjects during their conversation was Kaisa's love life. Sadly, she had little to report. Rose, who had married and had children late, thought Kaisa should find a man to spend the rest of her years with. As always, she didn't keep this opinion to herself and kept pestering Kaisa with it.

As it was, there had only been two men that she could report back about. One, a visiting Englishman, Kaisa had met at a tram stop in Helsinki a couple of years before. She'd been on the way home from her language class at FinnBrits when Henry had asked her if the tram they were waiting for would take him to Pasila Conference Centre. He was tall, a bit burly, but with pleasant pale blue eyes and greying dark brown hair. He was in Helsinki for the Slush conference, supporting a start-up in technology. With his ungloved hands and his ears red from the chill easterly winds that were whipping along the Helsinki streets that day, Henry had been freezing. Kaisa had found she felt sorry for him, and had agreed to sit next to the Englishman on the tram into town. Henry was an accountant, and after they'd spent the journey talking about the awful November weather in Helsinki, he'd invited Kaisa out to dinner. He'd laughed when Kaisa told him to buy a proper, warm coat, gloves and a woollen hat and ditch his Barbour jacket. After dinner that evening, as they stepped into a hail storm, Henry had told Kaisa he was married.

'I'm sorry,' Kaisa had replied. She'd shaken his hand and hadn't replied to any of the messages he sent her afterwards.

'You don't know the whole story!' both Rose and Tuuli had argued, but Kaisa's mind was made up. She'd not get into any relationship with a married man, whatever the circumstances.

The second 'almost relationship' was with a Swedish man whom Tuuli had introduced to Kaisa. Jonas was in banking and had worked with Tuuli when she'd briefly been with a Swedish corporation. He'd recently moved to Helsinki because of his job and had been divorced 'for years', as Tuuli put it. He and Kaisa had met at a drinks party at Tuuli's place, when she was celebrating her fiftieth birthday. Kaisa had spotted the tallish man standing on his own. Jonas had no hair, but he had full lips and pale blue eyes. His facial features were pretty, almost effeminate. When Tuuli introduced him to Kaisa, she was impressed by his strong handshake and the way he held her eye. Kaisa had smiled, and silently thanked Rosa for persuading her to wear a tight-fitting blue dress that complimented her figure and had a deep v-cut neckline, making her boobs look fuller than they actually were. A push-up bra helped, as did the high-heeled sandals, Kaisa thought, as she felt Jonas's eyes move over her body. The party had been full of couples, and Jonas and Kaisa soon realised they were the only two single people there.

'Do you have a feeling we might have been matched?' Jonas said. He had a pleasant twinkle in his eye, but Kaisa played at being horrified.

'I'm so sorry, I had no idea!' She hadn't flirted like this in years, or decades.

Jonas smiled, revealing an alarmingly white set of teeth. 'I don't mind in the least. In fact, I'm flattered,' he added.

Kaisa had had too many glasses of champagne to care one way or the other and spent the evening laughing at Jonas's jokes about golf – a sport he was passionate about. Kaisa played too, and hearing this, Jonas challenged her to a game.

When it was time to go home, Jonas offered to share a cab with Kaisa. In the back seat, he began kissing her, and when they arrived in Lauttasaari, Kaisa found herself inviting him in for a night cap. It was a Saturday night and Rosa was staying with a friend, so she didn't see the harm in it.

Jonas was very good in bed. Efficient, attentive and energetic, he covered all the bases. Kaisa hadn't had sex like that for years, and for the first time since Peter's death she felt something for another man. But it turned out sex was all they had in common. Jonas was a very competitive man. If he didn't win on the golf course, or if Rosa beat him at cards, or if Kaisa got a better score on the WiiFit tennis game she liked to play, Jonas would sulk. He'd even sulk if Kaisa didn't want to have sex. He took it as a personal failure if – on occasion – Kaisa didn't climax before he did. She tried to explain about the female body, but he wasn't interested. He'd failed and afterwards he'd not be in touch with Kaisa for weeks. In the end, one of these long periods of not seeing each other became a permanent parting of the ways.

Sometimes Kaisa missed Jonas and the sex, but she'd avoided the temptation to use him as just a booty call for now (Even if Tuuli had encouraged her to do just that).

NINE

As the army truck began its laborious journey up the mountainside, Kaisa was shaken out of her thoughts about her pathetic love life (or lack of it). The engine sounded as if it was struggling, and the uneven surface of the slope along the way meant all the passengers bumped into each other during the journey, which seemed to take forever. Looking at her watch when at last the vehicle stopped, she saw that just over ten minutes had passed. The driver helped each of the female passengers out of the truck, taking their hand and guiding them down the small step jutting out of the back of the vehicle. Kaisa noticed to her annoyance that he ignored the men, and let them hold onto the side of the platform instead. When it came to her turn, she said, looking at the rather handsome, archetypal blue-eyed Swede, 'Thank you, I'm fine.' The man dropped his hand and stretched his arm out to point to a path leading to the restaurant, which in the darkness she saw was a set of converted low-slung barns.

Inside, the place was dominated by a long table in the middle of the room, topped with a white linen tablecloth and silver cutlery. Traditional straw decorations hung from the ceiling. The lighting was subdued, with candles burning here and there, giving the whole place a warm, yellow glow. The smell of burning logs mingled with the appetising smell of cooking. Seasonal scents of ham, meatballs, pickled herring and smoked fish wafted in from somewhere.

'Beautiful,' Kaisa said and smiled at Tuuli. A young woman dressed in a red Christmas elf outfit greeted them with a broad smile. She was carrying a tray of *glögg* and offered them a glass. '*God Jul*,' she said and stretched her arm out to point Tuuli and Kaisa towards a large fireplace. 'Dinner will be served shortly.'

There were two other groups of people standing at the far end of the room, and the two friends nodded to them. Tuuli sipped her hot drink, her eyes surveying Kaisa from over the rim of her glass.

'What?' Kaisa said.

'You look nice,' Tuuli said.

Kaisa smiled and thanked her friend. She knew what Tuuli was getting at, but she wouldn't admit to anything. She knew herself that she'd made an effort today. Of course, it was Christmas Eve so she would normally have put on a nice dress. However, usually she'd be in the kitchen, cooking with Rosa for either Peter's parents, when on occasion they'd come to Helsinki to spend the holidays with them, or sometimes for her mother and her sister's family. More often lately it had just been Rosa and Grandma, or *Mummu* Pirjo, and her new husband, Rickard, though, as Tuuli often reminded Kaisa, Pirjo had been married to Rickard for twenty years now, so it was hardly a new relationship. The cooking was left to Kaisa, so by the time she sat down at the table, her make-up would be all but gone.

But today, she'd carefully applied her foundation, eyeshadow and mascara. She'd noticed as she put on her dark red velvet dress that her eyes shone more brightly then they had for some time. Being on the slopes had made her feel more alive, invigorated, and it showed in her complexion. Perhaps the massage with the sexy Niklas had also helped, Kaisa thought, unable to stop a smile forming on her lips. She'd also chosen to wear a set of large, fashionable pearls, which she knew suited her. She'd been shy to wear them, since they were rather showy, but they felt right for tonight, Christmas Eve, in a restaurant in the fashionable Swedish ski resort. Both Tuuli and Kaisa had decided to take a pair of smart shoes to change into, so they were both feeling rather fancy as they stood sipping their drinks.

'Does this remind you of anything?' Kaisa said and grinned.

'What?'

'Do you remember the Embassy party where I met Peter?'

Tuuli laughed, 'Not quite as posh, but yes, I see what you mean.'

Both women were quiet for a moment. Kaisa regretted mentioning Peter. It made her think about how she'd only been with him for a few years before he was taken away from her. However much she tried, she couldn't help reminiscing back to the wonderful evening at the British Embassy in Helsinki where they'd met. He'd been a newly qualified naval officer and she had been a student. They were so young, just twenty years old, but it had been love at first sight.

TEN

'Fancy seeing you two here!'

Kaisa was startled by the voice behind her.

Tom bent down and kissed Kaisa on the cheek. Even in her heels, Kaisa felt short next to him. His aftershave was something citrussy and she felt a frisson of excitement run through her body.

Tom was wearing a smart shirt and tie with a navy blazer and dark trousers. Kaisa glanced at his shoes, which were disappointingly casual. Not quite trainers, but some sort of comfortable-looking leather numbers.

Ricky also came and said hello, and the two men settled themselves next to the two friends.

How different this was to her usual Christmas Eve, Kaisa thought. Her body, although tired from the day's skiing, felt relaxed and she enjoyed basking in the attentions of the two 'Rich Boys', who were as charming as they had been long ago when the four of them first met.

'You both look absolutely lovely,' Ricky said, raising his glass and downing the red liquid in one go. 'How about we order something a little more festive?'

'Yes, please. This stuff is far too sweet.' Tuuli said, putting her half-full glass of mulled wine on the mantelpiece.

'Can we have a bottle of champagne, please?' Ricky said to the waiter, who was just passing them. While Ricky discussed the types of sparkling wines available, Tom glanced at Kaisa, raising his eyebrows. He bent down and whispered in her ear, ' 'Rich Boys', eh?'

Kaisa felt the heat of Tom's breath near her face, and when she turned, she found him so close that she could see the dark stubble on his chin. His lips were almost upon hers and she had to fight the urge to push her mouth against his. They stood there, Tom leaning towards her smiling, until Ricky cleared his throat loudly.

'Did you manage to choose a good bottle?' Tom said smiling, leaving Kaisa to catch her breath.

When the champagne arrived, and they'd all been handed a glass of the chilled bubbly, Ricky made a toast to 'Friendship'. The four smiled at each other. Kaisa took a large sip of the champagne and enjoyed the deliciously soft taste of the liquid. She wondered how much this decadent pleasure was costing, but decided not to care. They were with the 'Rich Boys' after all!

It was a wonderful evening. Kaisa laughed so much at Ricky and Tom's tall tales. She didn't realise that Tom was planning to move back to Finland, nor that Ricky had visited Tom often in Milan over the past thirty or so years. The restaurant staff had seated the four friends at the far end of the table, where they were served last, but where they were separate from the rest of the thirty or so guests. Ricky took charge of ordering the wines. They drank beer and schnapps with the marinated herring, French Sancerre with the fish course, and a deep red from Italy (Tom's choice) for the main course of ham, Jansson's Temptation, meatballs and reindeer stew.

Afterwards Tom ordered another bottle of champagne for the coffee and pudding, after which it was time to catch the army truck back to the main road, where taxis waited for the guests. As they were getting out of the truck, Tom offered Kaisa his hand, his white teeth smiling against the darkness. His touch was warm, and as her feet hit the snowy road, Tom continued to hold her.

'It's slippery,' he said, offering his arm.

'Thank you,' she replied, and they began walking towards the headlights of the waiting cars.

'A nightcap at ours?' Kaisa heard Tuuli ask behind her.

'Excellent plan!' Ricky said, and Tom, leaning in to talk to Kaisa quietly, said, 'If it's OK with you?'

Kaisa looked up at Tom's face, trying to make out his expression. His full lips were slightly upturned at the corners, but his eyes were serious. Kaisa nodded. She felt safe in the knowledge that Tom didn't really fancy her; he was just being a good friend and there was nothing against that on Christmas Eve, now was there? Then she thought of something, 'How are you going to get back to your hotel?'

Tom looked quietly at her for a moment, then replied, 'We'll walk.'

Kaisa nodded. She recalled that the road wound its way from their chalet all the way up to Fjällgården. It was a long uphill walk, but if you were warmly dressed, it would be fine and only take twenty minutes or so. She noticed that their steps fell in line as they made their way down the hill.

ELEVEN

W hen they entered the apartment in Tottbacken, Ricky gave a low whistle. 'Not bad!'

The living quarters of the three-bedroomed apartment were impressive. The lounge faced the village in one direction and the ski slopes in the other. The room had a pale oak interior, with a vast, stone-faced open fire by the wall between full-height windows. Outside you could make out the snowy roofs of the houses in the valley below, interspersed with Christmas lights, all of which looked spell-binding against the blackness of the sky beyond. Kaisa just couldn't get enough of the view. The sofa in a grey shade echoed the hue of the fireplace, and the two comfy chairs in red gave the room a pop of colour. The open-plan kitchen had black marble worktops and spot lighting above. Everything had an air of luxury about it, even down to the evenly chopped logs beautifully arranged in an expensive-looking hemp basket next to the fireplace.

Tuuli giggled and took Ricky's arm while throwing her boots and coat off. Standing in the doorway, sensing Tom behind her, Kaisa realised her friend was quite drunk.

'I'm getting a bottle of champagne!' Tuuli shouted, opening the large stainless-steel fridge door, while Ricky went to the door leading to the balcony to admire the view. Kaisa turned to face Tom, who shrugged his shoulders, lifting the corners of his mouth into a smile. A strange sensation in Kaisa's chest suddenly made it hard to breathe.

'I'll be just a moment,' she said, making her way to her bedroom and the en-suite bathroom. She closed the door and stood looking at herself in the mirror above the designer sink. The bathroom was all black marble and white porcelain, with the shiny steel of the shower enclosure and the fancy towel rail reflected in the overhead spotlights. It must be a flattering light, she thought, looking at herself. She appeared more youthful. Her cheeks were rosy from the cold air outside, and her eyes seemed bluer and clearer than they did at home in rainy Helsinki. Even her hair, which usually became electric and impossible to handle in low temperatures, seemed glossy and very blonde. She'd had the foresight to visit both her hairdresser and beauty parlour before the holiday. Her eyebrows, slightly tinted, looked tidy and seemed to accentuate her eyes. Kaisa added a little lipstick, flushed the loo, and washed her hands, for appearance's sake. (She wasn't sure if she could be heard from the rest of the apartment.)

When Kaisa stepped into the living room, she saw Tom sitting in one of the comfy chairs, sipping a glass of champagne. Another glass was poured and set on a table between the sofa and the chairs. She looked at Tom, who lifted his glass, gazing at her eyes. Kaisa glanced behind her, just in case she had missed Tuuli or Ricky in the small kitchen area, but they were nowhere to be seen.

'I think Tuuli was feeling a little tired,' Tom said. His face was serious; there wasn't a hint of a smile, or innuendo, there.

'And I guess Ricky went to make sure she got to bed OK?' Kaisa said, trying to keep a straight face. She sat down in front of Tom and raised her champagne flute.

'Well, Happy Christmas again!'

Tom lifted his glass and his face broke into a wide smile. They both burst out laughing.

'She's impossible!' Kaisa said between bouts of

giggling. 'You know that one time she got me in trouble with my daughter's babysitter by telling her I'd not be home that night because I had a date!'

Kaisa remembered the time when Rosa had been six or seven years old, and Tuuli had organised another of her blind dates for her. She'd whisked Kaisa off to the hairdressers straight from work, told her she would fetch Rosa from school and brief the babysitter. The date had been a complete disaster, so Kaisa had arrived home early, only to be met with a teenage couple making out in her living room.

Tom laughed and finished his drink. 'I guess it's time for me to walk up the hill.' He got up, but just then a bubbling noise and steam came from the balcony. 'What the ...' he said and went to open the door.

'Oh no, she's fired up the Jacuzzi!'

Tom turned around and nearly hit Kaisa with his arm.

'There's a Jacuzzi?'

TWELVE

T om couldn't afterwards remember whose idea it had been to get into the hot tub, but suddenly there they were, just the two of them, with the water bubbling around them and steam rising into the freezing night, drinking champagne. Below them was Åre village, and in the distance the lake, shrouded in darkness. The tips of Kaisa's hair were wet on her shoulders and she was smiling at him.

'I'm quite drunk,' she giggled. She was wearing a black swimming costume with a v-shape cutting into her cleavage. Tom had to admit she looked good for her age. His ex, who was Italian, was ten years younger but looked weathered. She was slim but had been smoking all her life, so her face and body were lined and leathery. Tom shivered.

'You cold?' Kaisa asked.

'No, no, just thinking about my ex.'

'Oh,' Kaisa gazed at him. Her eyes had a searching look and Tom remembered what it was that had so attracted him to this Finnish-speaking girl all those years ago. Kaisa had a nice figure, blonde hair and blue eyes, but she hadn't been the prettiest girl in Hanken by far. She was different, somehow. There was something in her eyes, a vulnerability combined with a depth, that drew him to her. She had looked at him then, when he'd first spoken to her, as she did now, intently, as if there was a passion inside of her just dying to get out.

Passion.

Oh, God, Tom needed passion. He could not remember the last time he'd felt that with a woman. Yes, he'd had women alright, too many of them, but so often sex with them had just been a release, a necessity of life. What was it about women these days that they had such a hard time enjoying sex simply for the sake of enjoying it? There always had to be complications, relationships, promises of dinners, keeping in touch, or of 'just some time to spend together' as one thirty-year-old Swedish web designer had put it. That relationship had ended abruptly two years ago, when Tom had forgotten to text her on her birthday. How was he supposed to remember the date when they'd only known each other for a matter of months?

'I don't want to think about her,' Tom now said, and he leaned over the tub to clink glasses with Kaisa. As he did so, however, he slipped, and fell towards Kaisa. To avoid hitting her face with his glass, he put one arm forward next to her left shoulder and ended up kneeling down between her legs.

'Oops,' she said and gave her most charming smile.

Tom felt her knees tighten around his hips. If that wasn't an invitation, Tom didn't know what was. He gazed at her eyes and saw how pink and wet her lips were. He took her glass from her. Stretching over, he placed both flutes down on the side and settled back in the same spot, held by Kaisa's long legs under the warm, bubbling water.

'*Posso baciarti?*' he said hoarsely in Italian. He remembered how Kaisa had liked him speaking Italian to her. He felt himself get hard.

Kaisa lifted up her eyes and gave him a look that screamed 'Yes'. He bent down to kiss her mouth. He held her head gently at first, carefully placing his hands on either side of her face, but then he lowered them to her waist and pulled Kaisa towards him. They moved into the middle of the tub, where he pushed his tongue inside her mouth. Feeling Kaisa's hips against his erection, he let his hands drop down to her bottom and lifted her legs up. She wrapped them around his body and they tumbled backwards against the other end of the Jacuzzi. He let go of her and she floated away, laughing.

'I don't think this is the best place for this, is it?' she said, giving him a look that was pure lust. Tom pulled Kaisa towards him again and kissed her once more, this time for longer, less hurriedly. When he let go of her again, he noticed there was a snowflake, a tiny crystal, attached to one of her eyelashes. He looked up to the sky and saw the fluffy, white slivers falling silently down on top of them.

'It's snowing!' Kaisa whispered, following his gaze. Her eyes travelled back to Tom. 'Shall we go inside?' he said quietly.

THIRTEEN

K aisa woke to an empty space next to her. She reached across to feel Tom's warmth and found the bed was cold. Her mouth was dry and she pulled the duvet up to cover her face when she remembered what had happened the night before. It seems Tom had got over his little problem, she thought, and she smiled to herself. The sex had been good, they were comfortable with each other, and he'd liked the things she had done to him. There had also been passion, she'd seen it in his eyes, in the way he kept stroking her body, and in the intense looks he gave her. And from time to time he'd spoken to her in Italian, which had just been the most sexy thing she'd ever heard. His ex was Italian, but that was something Kaisa didn't wish to consider this morning (was it her he had been making love to last night?). She cast the thoughts of Tom's other women away too. She could only guess at the number there had been.

Don't think about them.

Instead, she recalled how she hadn't thought of Peter once during their love-making last night. As she pushed her legs out of bed, she saw a note on the pillow next to her.

Sorry I couldn't stay. Thought it best to go back to the hotel. I had fun, see you later on the slopes today?

Tom

Kaisa turned the piece of paper over in her hands and reread it.

Fun. He'd had 'fun'.

Was there anything wrong with that? Kaisa, too had had fun, but ...

Don't overthink it!

Kaisa could hear Tuuli's voice in her head, but as she got into the shower, she couldn't let go of the feeling that there was something wrong with the note. Was what happened the night before just a one-night stand to Tom? Was she just someone to have 'fun' with? Suddenly, as the warm water ran down her face and body, she realised she was angry. And hurt. Even if this was only a holiday romance, there was no need to spell it out so clearly!

Tom was obviously exactly what she'd always thought he was – a man who still, at the age of sixty, was unable to make a commitment.

A commitment? Was that what she wanted?

No, Kaisa wasn't looking for a permanent relationship. She'd long ago accepted that she may be lonely in her later years. Luckily, for now, her mother lived in Helsinki and was still in very good health. And although her sister Sirkka and her family lived up in Lapland, she was very close to her. Then there was Rosa. She hoped her daughter would stay in Helsinki, even if she got a place of her own, as she often threatened to do.

Kaisa had come on this Christmas break to have a different kind of holiday, to have fun, yes, but she'd never imagined that would involve a holiday romance. Besides, it would have been different if it had been with someone she'd never met before, or would never see again. She and Tom had history, and it was more than likely that they would meet again through Tuuli and Ricky. Now they'd so obviously buried the hatchet, Ricky and Tuuli must know about it. It would be impossible to say 'No' to any future get-togethers.

What a mess she'd got into.

Kaisa dried herself and dressed for a day on the slopes. What the hell, be what may, she thought. If Tom just wanted to have fun, so be it. She'll have fun with him, but she'll not go to bed with him again. That was a one-off.

Another thought entered Kaisa's mind as she brushed her teeth. Had Tom slept with her just to wipe away the embarrassment of their unsuccessful night all those years ago in Helsinki? To stroke his enormous ego? And to show her, Kaisa, that he was a pure-blooded man after all? Anger surged inside Kaisa's chest again, as she spat out the toothpaste and water, and gazed at herself in the bathroom mirror.

Looking at her reflection, which showed her eyes wider and darker than they usually were, she decided Tom was not worth her fury. She'd be as nice as anything to him today on the slopes, and for the rest of their time in the ski resort. She'd not give him the satisfaction of thinking that last night had meant anything to her. Which, she decided, it had not.

When Kaisa stepped inside the living area, Ricky and Tuuli were sitting at the table having breakfast.

'Sleep well?' Tuuli asked.

Kaisa nodded, keeping her eyes on Tuuli, but her friend's expression was the same as usual. She sat down opposite Ricky, keeping an eye on him too, but he just smiled at her briefly. He was leafing through a newspaper, wearing his reading glasses. Perhaps they didn't know Tom had been in her bed? Kaisa glanced over to the hot tub on the balcony, and saw that the cover had been replaced and the Jacuzzi had been turned off. She glanced at the kitchen top and saw two champagne flutes, washed and rinsed, drying next to the sink. Tom must have tidied up before he left. Thankfully, the snowfall in the night had been heavy and the hot tub was covered with a thick layer of white, like a cake with a generous helping of icing, burying any signs of her and Tom's activities last night.

What am I worrying about? This was what Tuuli and possibly Ricky had planned, had wanted, wasn't it?

Yet, Kaisa felt embarrassed. Even though she knew Tom from before, now their love-making – or the 'fun' sex they'd had last night – seemed wrong somehow. It seemed too soon, as if she'd gone to bed with a man on a first date. Which was not true, of course. After years of flirting as students in the corridors of their university, Tom and Kaisa eventually went on a date – two dates if you counted the chance meeting and lunch they'd had in the aftermath of Kaisa and Peter's separation. A week or so after that meeting, Kaisa had accepted a dinner invitation to Tom's penthouse apartment in Ullanlinna, where their affair, if you could call it that, had come to an abrupt end. Tom had asked Kaisa not to breathe a word about the evening to anyone, but Kaisa had not been able to hide it from Tuuli. She knew her friend could keep a secret, and over all these years, she'd been true to her word. Now, however, watching Tuuli's back as she stood by the kitchen counter, Kaisa regretted that she'd told her friend about Tom's failure in bed. Tuuli was so close to Ricky that she must have confided in him, mustn't she?

'I've got a bit of a fuzzy head, though,' Kaisa said, addressing her friend, who was busy with the Nespresso machine, and not looking at Kaisa.

'Due to the copious amounts of booze we had last night, no doubt,' Kaisa added, giving a small laugh, testing Tuuli and Ricky a little more.

'Yeah,' Tuuli said without turning to face Kaisa. Giving Kaisa a quick smile, Ricky muttered, 'It is Christmas!' He continued to look at Kaisa over the top of his glasses and added, 'Fresh snow today, should be good skiing. You up for it?'

Kaisa nodded. It was evident they had no idea

about what had happened between her and Tom last night.

'Coffee?' Tuuli placed a cup in front of Kaisa and sat down. 'That bloody machine is difficult to operate! What's wrong with an old-fashioned percolator, eh?

FOURTEEN

Kaisa spotted Tom first. She saw a figure in a grey snowsuit with red stripes moving fast down the piste. He was wearing a pair of red-tinted goggles over a grey helmet. Something about the movements of the lean, strong body convinced Kaisa that the competent-looking skier moving towards them at speed was Tom.

'There he is!' she said and pointed towards the figure in the distance.

Ricky, Tuuli and Kaisa were standing by the Kabinbanan, waiting to board the gondola to the topmost pistes in the Swedish ski resort.

Ricky glanced at his watch. 'He's late.'

Kaisa had the urge to spring to Tom's defence. They'd been waiting for over ten minutes, that was true, but she knew it was difficult to time a rendezvous on the slopes. You never knew if a lift somewhere along the way would stop when you were dangling on a chair above a piste, freezing your bones off. Kaisa, Ricky and Tuuli had ordered a cab from Tottbacken, stopping en route at Ricky and Tom's hotel to pick up Ricky's snowsuit, skies and boots, whereas Tom had already been up on the slopes for hours. It was now 1 pm and the friends had decided to take the gondola up, have lunch and then ski back down to Fjällgården to spend the remaining hours of the day in the boy's hotel, which was also close to Kaisa and Tuuli's chalet on the eastern side of the mountain.

But Kaisa remained silent. She needed to watch what she said and to remain as jolly and friendly as she'd been the night before. She tried to steady her anticipation as the grey ski-suited figure came closer.

Why was she so nervous?

Tom slowed down as the hill flattened close to the lifts. He stopped smartly in front of the group of friends and smiled, lifting his goggles over his helmet.

'*Ciao!*' he said, looking at Kaisa.

'Hi,' Kaisa replied, feeling shy, and gazing down at her boots.

Tuuli and Ricky both glanced at Kaisa, but Tom interrupted them.

'It's fantastic up there! The sun is out and the new powder is amazing.'

'C'mon let's go,' Ricky said, somewhat impatiently, Kaisa thought, and the four of them made their way towards the gondola. There were many people rushing to get onto the carriages as they moved slowly along the platform. Tom and Kaisa were pushed back by an eager group of youngsters and ended up missing the carriage Ricky and Tuuli had entered.

'We'll see you at the top!' Ricky shouted to Tom and Kaisa just as the doors closed and the gondola jerked upwards.

Once they were settled into their carriage, Tom said, 'How are you this morning?'

He was standing close to Kaisa. They'd been pushed together by the other skiers, who were mostly about Rosa's age. Suddenly Kaisa felt very old.

Too old to be having butterflies in your stomach because a man you made love to drunkenly last night is standing too close to you. Pull yourself together!

'Fine,' Kaisa replied and lifted her head up to look at Tom. She saw that his lips were curled into a smile and his eyes were shining.

His gaze was intent. 'Just fine? I hoped you'd be feeling better than "fine"!'

Kaisa felt the blood rush to her face and was sure

she'd blushed. She glanced around her but the other skiers were interested only in each other, not the two 'oldies' having a discussion about last night's amorous activities.

I don't suppose they think we do it anymore, she mused to herself. She could feel a wide smile over-taking her face.

'What's so funny?' Tom asked.

'Oh, nothing,' Kaisa said. She lifted her eyes towards Tom once more and said, hearing the sarcasm in her voice too late, 'Well. It was "fun".'

She had just enough time to see Tom's expression change and his face fall before the gondola shifted and rocked. They'd arrived at Åreskutan, the top of the mountain.

Tuuli and Kaisa had planned to have dinner in the apartment on Christmas Day. Kaisa had managed to order a turkey and vegetables from the local store and had volunteered to be chef. That morning, before leaving for the slopes, she'd prepared the bird, covered it with strips of bacon, and put it in the oven. Every year since moving back to Finland, she'd had an English Christmas Day lunch. Tuuli had joined Rosa and her for the meal most years, and sometimes, if Peter's parents were visiting, they'd bring English fare such as pork sausages wrapped in bacon, proper Christmas pudding, minced pies and cranberry sauce. This year, it would have to be a pared down version, but Kaisa didn't mind. She'd planned not to do it, but Tuuli had persuaded her. Now, of course, Ricky had invited himself along, and Kaisa assumed that meant Tom would be there too.

'You don't mind we're having them over tonight, do you?' Tuuli whispered to Kaisa at the top of the mountain, after the boys had scooted off down, shouting for Tuuli and Kaisa to follow their lead. 'Tom can have the spare room.'

'No, no, not at all,' Kaisa said, and she pushed down with her sticks, accelerating her downhill glide. The snow was as good as it looked; up here on the top, the wide piste still had some virgin areas where no one had skied before. The snowfall had been heavy last night, and not many people had bothered to come up to the top. It was bitterly cold, with a northerly wind that whipped across the mountain, leaving a thin layer of dry, powdery snow on top of the piste. Kaisa moved in a regular pattern, carefully choosing the point where she was going to turn and avoiding the tracks created by other skiers. Suddenly she heard a swish and saw Tuuli overtaking her, gesturing a greeting with her pole. To catch up, Kaisa sped up, no longer caring where she turned. Her heart pumped in her ears, and she very nearly missed Tuuli, Ricky and Tom, who'd stopped at the top of a small hill. Kaisa turned her skies diagonally against the mountain, sending a snow flurry over Tom, who was the one standing nearest to her.

'Sorry!' Kaisa said and laughed. 'I didn't mean to get you.'

'Looking good, Miss England,' Ricky said and nudged Tom, who lost his balance. He tumbled against Kaisa, who caught his sleeve.

Tom dusted himself off. 'Watch it!'

'Thank you, Kaisa. And I apologise for the childish behaviour of my friend here,' Tom said. Although they were both wearing goggles, Kaisa could see Tom's eyes burning into her. In spite of what she had decided, his physical presence did make her heart beat faster.

'Tuuli and I want to take another trip up to the top on the gondola. You coming, Kaisa?' Ricky asked.

Not looking at Tom, Kaisa said, 'You guys go on. I think I've had enough for today. I'll make my way home and get on with dinner.'

'Tom?' Ricky asked, and to her surprise, Tom said, 'You go on, I'm a bit knackered too. I'd already been up and down twice before you sleepyheads joined me.' He was grinning at the others.

'We feel very bad,' Ricky said and flicked his pole at Tom's legs.

'Why don't we meet in an hour or so at Fjällgården?' Tuuli said. 'You two can get the beers in? Don't want you to go home and cook, Kaisa! It's a holiday and the bird can look after itself, can't it?'

'True,' Kaisa said. She'd put the turkey in the oven at a very low temperature; it wouldn't be ready until late afternoon. After Ricky and Tuuli had disappeared below the little ledge of snow they were standing on, Kaisa glanced at Tom, who said, 'Why don't we stop off at Hummelstugan first? It's just down there.' He pointed into the distance. Kaisa was fully aware of Hummelstugan's location and had planned to stop in the mountain restaurant herself for a breather. She was tired; she wasn't used to such intense physical exercise every day, and it would take at least another thirty minutes to ski back to the men's hotel bar.

'Sure,' she replied. 'After you,' she added, and pointed her stick at the piste. She didn't want Tom to watch her ski. She knew she was the least experienced of them all, and felt self-conscious in front of Tom, who was the best skier in the group. That was the only reason she didn't want him to follow her, she told herself, as she set off behind him, aware that he'd obviously slowed his pace to Kaisa's.

FIFTEEN

Hummelstugan was busy. A lot of skiers had decided to congregate at the Alpine-style cafe and restaurant, with its impressive view of the valley and Lake Åre below, and inside there was a queue. Tom, who'd opened the heavy doors for Kaisa in a gentlemanly manner, immediately grew impatient behind her and asked to talk to 'someone in charge'. A pretty young woman in pigtails approached them and somehow Tom managed to get her to give them table in the restaurant by the corner window.

'Not too bad a view, is it?' he said. His face looked ruddy with a few red patches from the chill, and his hair was mussed up. She had to admit he looked good. Kaisa noticed that most women had given him a second, and even a third, glance as she and Tom had passed the queue and made their way to the table.

Kaisa touched her hair to pat it down a little. Her cheeks felt hot; she too must have looked flushed.

'What about a bottle of the good stuff?' Tom said. He was glancing at the menu the waitress had given them. 'And look, they have scallops! Do you like seafood?' he added and looked directly at Kaisa.

Kaisa had to giggle; this was such archetypal 'Rich Boy' behaviour that she couldn't control herself.

Tom got the gist, 'C'mon, we have something to celebrate, don't we?'

'Do we?' Kaisa said, trying to look serious. But before she could say anything more, the waitress was at their table, ready to take their order.

'How am I supposed to get down that mountain after this?' she asked when a bottle of Moet in an ice bucket and two glasses arrived. It seemed that ordering champagne on Christmas Day on the Swedish Alps was a common occurrence, because the waitress hadn't batted an eyelid.

'I can take you between my legs. I've done it before.' Tom said and lifted his glass. He had a mischievous look in his eye.

Kaisa clinked glasses with him and shook her head.

There was a silence as Kaisa, with difficulty, took

her eyes off Tom for a moment and admired the view. In the distance, the white lake snaked through the valley; to the right, a four-seater lift dropped skiers in front of the restaurant. The slope ran on the other side of the building, leaving a steep off-piste area where two young boys were making slow progress down the mountainside.

'I bet they regret that hasty decision now,' Tom said, reading her thoughts.

'Yeah,' Kaisa replied, sipping her drink. 'You have sons. Did they do stupid things when they were younger?'

'They did, often encouraged by their dad, I'm afraid,' Tom said, giving a dry laugh. He was looking down at his hands resting on the white tablecloth.

Without thinking, Kaisa stretched her hand out and placed her fingers on the back of Tom's palm. Her touch made Tom look up. Seeing sadness, Kaisa squeezed his hand harder.

'You OK?'

'Sorry,' Tom said, finishing his glass of champagne. He released his hands from Kaisa's grip and nodding to her half-full glass, 'Top up?'

She nodded. Carefully, tipping the glass, so that the bubbles wouldn't spill over the rim, he poured more champagne for them both. Kaisa noticed how white and neat his nails were. She wondered if he had them manicured in Milan.

'I was thinking about my mother,' he said after replacing the bottle in the silver ice bucket. He wasn't looking at Kaisa but was stroking the table-cloth in front of him.

'Tuuli told me. I'm so sorry,' Kaisa said quietly.

Tom lifted his eyes and told her how his mother had been full of life, stylish to the end, and didn't want to accept her illness. Kaisa didn't ask what this had been but surmised from Tom's words that it must have been cancer or something that had spread quickly and taken her suddenly. The way Tom spoke about his mother made her think about the Italian café she'd worked in London while trying to get her career going in journalism, and how the family who owned and ran it had treated 'la Mamma'. The tenderness and respect they afforded their mother and grandmother was something special.

Their food came, and for a few moments Kaisa and Tom ate in silence.

'This is very good,' Kaisa said after a while. The scallops were cooked to perfection. They were served with buttery mash, some leafy greens, and there was a sauce of some kind on top, which Kaisa tried to avoid because she knew it probably contained nothing more than cream and butter. But she ate heartily all the same; she hadn't realised how hungry she'd been. She noticed that Tom must have been equally ravenous because he'd already wolfed down his portion. Kaisa offered the rest of her potato mash to Tom, who, after a brief hesitation, grinned and ate her plate clean too.

By the time they were perusing the dessert menus and finishing the champagne, Kaisa felt relaxed and happy. She surveyed Tom and smiled at him when he suggested they have all three desserts on the menu because he couldn't decide which one he preferred.

'I'm so full I don't think I can manage any at all,' Kaisa laughed.

Tom leaned over the table. 'You'll burn it all off later, I promise.'

SIXTEEN

'And where have you two been?' Tuuli said when Tom and Kaisa finally made it to the Fjällgården bar. She actually winked at her friend, but Kaisa just gave her a wide smile. The ski back from Hummelstugan had been a lot easier than Kaisa had anticipated, and she'd even kept up with Tom's speed. They'd skied non-stop, with Kaisa following Tom, who every now and then glanced backwards to make sure she was still there. It made Kaisa think that he really did care for her. Perhaps she'd misunderstood the note?

When they stopped at the hotel entrance, Tom had swept her into his arms and given her a quick kiss. Kaisa couldn't help but fall into his arms, happy and exhilarated from the best skiing she'd ever managed in her life.

The bar was heaving; there was a live band and they had to shout to each other in order to be heard. It took Tom and Kaisa a while to find Ricky and Tuuli, who'd managed to get a booth in the depths of the hotel bar, right next to the dance floor. The band was playing 1980s music, with people dancing slowly in their ski-boots.

'Like old times,' isn't it? Tom said, shouting into her ear.

Kaisa smiled and removed her ski jacket and loosened her boots. Ricky had got them a bottle of champagne – again – and they clinked their glasses.

'To the best Christmas ever,' Tom said.

The band began playing old Swedish classics, songs they'd all listened and danced to in Hanken.

'Shall we?' Tom said, when the female vocalist began singing the first chords of Eva Dahlgren's hit, 'Who lights the stars'. Kaisa looked at Tom, who was standing in front of her with an outstretched hand, and then glanced down at her boots.

Tom followed Kaisa's eyes.

'It's OK, it's a slow one, I'll make sure you don't fall.'

Kaisa nodded and, as she got up, looked over to Tuuli, who raised her eyebrows. Kaisa gave her a smile and took Tom's hand.

It was three seconds of eternity,
Three short breaths.

Of all these encounters,
And everything
that should have happened.

How rarely I am the reason
Why life turns around.

But who turns the winds?
Who makes me go
Where I've never gone before?

Who lights the stars
That I only see in your eyes?

Who turns the winds
And brings me thoughts
I've never had before?

Kaisa had always loved the poignant lyrics of Eva Dahlgren's songs, but this tune was her absolute favourite. She'd listened to this song a lot in the year she'd come back from London. It was as if Eva was singing to her. Her life up to that point, before she'd made the positive decision to leave England and return home, had been full of coincidences beyond her control. But now, listening to the song for the first time in years, leaning into Tom's broad shoulders, and taking in his manly scent, mixed with a citrussy aftershave, she saw that there was such a thing as serendipity. 'All those encounters,' she thought to herself, they all meant something.

When the slow piece had finished, Tom looked into her eyes and smiled.

'You liked that?'

Kaisa nodded and returned his smile.

Suddenly the band struck a chord and began playing a classic party song by Tomas Ledin that the Hanken disco had often played at the start of an evening. Tom let Kaisa go, and as much as they could, in the clunky ski boots, they danced, laughing so much that occasionally one of them would lose their balance.

'Please, I can't take any more,' Kaisa said after she'd fallen into Tom's arms a second time. With his hand around her waist, Tom led Kaisa back to the table, where Ricky and Tuuli were watching. For a moment, Kaisa felt self-conscious, but she couldn't keep the wide the smile off her face.

'Can't believe they are playing that old song!'

Kaisa said loudly, trying to be heard over the noise of the music and the clattering sound of people dancing in their boots. She settled herself next to Tuuli, who filled her glass. The bottle was finished. 'Shall we get another one?' Tuuli asked.

Kaisa glanced at her watch and saw it was past 4pm.

'Oh my God, the turkey!'

SEVENTEEN

Tom had never eaten English Christmas food before. He'd been to London a few times, particularly in the eighties, just before he moved back to Italy.

Once, he'd thought about Kaisa and had even looked her up in the telephone directory, but seeing she was listed under 'Peter and Kaisa Williams', had decided not to call her. That was when he'd given up on her. How wrong he'd been not to consider her before! Oh well, there was no point in regretting the past. She was here now, sitting opposite him, looking gorgeous. He couldn't take his eyes off her, even if he knew the way they'd behaved today together would make Ricky say, 'I told you so', about two million times.

Spending the night with her, and then talking to her today in Hummelstugan, and dancing with her to the old, old tracks, he'd realised how similar they were, and how much he really had been smitten with her in Hanken all those years ago. It was no use thinking back, but why had he been so stupid not to pursue her harder then? Tom shook his head, a physical gesture to get away from regrets. Perhaps now that they were both older, they would enjoy each other more. He thought back to the way she'd looked at him in the Jacuzzi, the snowflakes settling on her eyelashes. And later, the way her long legs gripped his waist.

He'd watched her sleep for a moment before he'd left the flat that morning. He was always an early riser these days, but he didn't want to disturb Kaisa, who'd looked so peaceful with her hands tucked under her chin and her blonde hair spread out on the pillow. He'd fought the urge to kiss her, and instead tiptoed out of the flat, leaving the note.

'You enjoying it?' Kaisa asked, nodding to the plate in front of Tom.

'Hmm, yes, the turkey is lovely,' he replied.

He could see Tuuli and Ricky exchange glances, but he didn't want to say anything to embarrass Kaisa. Besides, they'd spent less than forty-eight hours together. It was early days. And there was something he needed to sort out first.

But Kaisa beat him to it. Addressing Tuuli and Ricky, and raising her glass of red wine, she said, 'Don't look so smug you two. It seems Tom and I do have something in common and enjoy each other's company.' Here Kaisa glanced at Tom, and smiled. 'So stop sniggering like a couple of teenagers and let's have another great evening?'

'I drink to that,' Tom said, and Tuuli and Ricky jointly murmured their assent.

'I'm just so pleased,' Tuuli said later when she and Kaisa were trying to produce some coffee out of the Nespresso machine. The men had gone to the living-room and were inspecting the workings of the DVD machine. Ricky had suggested a film – he'd seen there was a whole library of them in the chalet. Tuuli put her hand on Kaisa's arm, 'You deserve a bit of happiness.'

Kaisa could see that her friend's eyes were damp, so she pulled Tuuli towards her and the two hugged hard.

'It's early days, though, you know,' Kaisa said.

'I know, I know,' Tuuli replied.

'But,' Kaisa added in a low voice, looking over to

where Ricky and Tom were pushing buttons on a remote and seeing the effect of their actions on the screen. 'It does feel so right.'

'Aww,' Tuuli exclaimed.

'Shh, don't. I don't want to jinx it.'

'Of course,' Tuuli nodded. Then, after managing to produce a small cup of espresso, she prodded Kaisa's side with her elbow. 'So, tell me, have you two done it yet?'

Kaisa smiled at her friend and nodded.

Tuuli placed a hand over her open mouth. She glanced into the living room, but the men's attention was still on the large TV screen.

'A Kiss?'

'Yeeees,' Kaisa said, and now she couldn't keep her face straight.

'And more?'

'Uh-huh.'

'You didn't!' Tuuli said, again raising her voice. 'Last night?'

'Yes, but keep your voice down.' Again Kaisa tried to assume a serious face but couldn't. She didn't realise how much she'd wanted to tell her friend about the previous night.

'And it was good?'

'Yes,' Kaisa said, lowering her eyes. After all these

years, she was still not comfortable talking about sex with anyone.

Tuuli took Kaisa into her embrace, and whispered into her ear.

'I am so happy. And you, remember to be happy too.'

EIGHTEEN

That evening, after they'd watched a Swedish film, *A Man Called Ove*, which none of them had seen before, Tuuli pulled Ricky off the sofa and said, 'I'm tired, time for bed.' She looked over at Kaisa, who feared her friend was going to wink at her, but she didn't. Instead, she kissed Kaisa on the cheek and said, 'What time do you want to go up the mountain tomorrow? The weather forecast is quite good again, so we could make it a bit earlier than today.'

Tom, who'd stretched his long legs out on one of the comfy chairs next to Kaisa, said, 'Not lunchtime, you mean?'

'Cheeky,' Tuuli replied. 'We're on holiday, so we're doing as we please, isn't that right, Kaisa?' Kaisa tried to look demure, 'I'm all for setting off a bit earlier. Take advantage of the freshly prepared pistes.'

The snowplough had just started its laborious work, flattening the day's humps and bumps, on the slope outside their chalet.

'This really is a fantastic location, thank you for brining me here,' Kaisa said and gazed at Tuuli.

'My pleasure,' her friend added and waved good-night to her and Tom. 'I'll aim to be at breakfast around nine, then?'

'Sounds good,' Kaisa replied.

When they were alone at last, Tom got up and pulled Kaisa close to him. He glanced over to where the door to the hall had just been closed by Ricky and then reached out for Kaisa's hand. He put her palm against his mouth, keeping his eyes fixed on hers. Running the fingers of his other hand along her cheek, he said, 'Can I kiss you?'

Kaisa nodded and lifted her face up to him. Finally, Tom thought, as he tasted the soft flesh of Kaisa's lips. He pushed his tongue inside her and pulled her closer. Kaisa let out a sound, a whisper really, and that made Tom want her even more.

'Can I stay tonight?' he said, after he'd pulled himself away.

Kaisa nodded, and bringing his mouth towards her, kissed him. Then, sliding her arm around his waist, she led him to her room.

NINETEEN

The next day, at breakfast, neither Ricky or Tuuli made any comment about Tom's presence. They discussed the practicalities of how they were going to meet later, because both men had left their ski gear at the hotel before coming over to the apartment. Without a sideways glance from either of them, they ate and agreed to meet outside the Fjällgården later.

Kaisa had told Tom last night that Tuuli knew they'd got together. They'd been lying in bed, Kaisa in the crook of his arm. She'd felt his body move as she spoke, and when she looked up, she saw he was nodding. He hadn't said anything though. Kaisa was a little worried about the lack of reaction, so she'd added, 'It just makes it easier. I'm not saying that I'm expecting this is anything more than ...'

'Shhh,' Tom had said, pulling himself up and placing a finger on her mouth. He'd looked at Kaisa with those dark eyes of his, his hair flopping over them, and said, 'This is the best Christmas I've ever had.'

'Me too,' Kaisa had replied.

Later, after they'd made their way to Fjällgården, they took the six-seater up to Sadeln, an easier ski area close to the men's hotel and their own apartment. On the lift, Kaisa ended up sitting next to Tom again, but with Tuuli on her other side. The wind around the eastern side of the mountain was even fiercer than it had been the previous day and the friends adjusted their clothing to cover up as much of their face and body as possible. Kaisa could feel Tom's strong legs next to hers and she turned her head towards him. He removed his leather ski glove and squeezed her thigh.

The lift slowed down and the four friends got off, skidding on a piece of ice that had formed at the point where the skiers dismounted. Kaisa struggled with her balance, and would have toppled over but for Tom, who was right next to her and took hold of her elbow. He led her away from the next lot of skiers gliding down from the lift.

'Thank you,' Kaisa said, embarrassed. It was such a rookie mistake, to lose your balance getting off a lift.

'You OK?' Tom said, letting go of Kaisa.

She nodded and glanced towards two shapes further away. Ricky and Tuuli were waiting at the top of the piste, facing Lake Åre. The view was breathtaking. The sun was behind a hazy layer of clouds, its faint rays creating a pale glow over the horizon. The slope veered down towards the woods and beyond the white shape of the lake meandered between the dark pine trees. A couple of skiers were making their way down the slope, but then there was a lull, and the piste was empty.

'Let's get going before we freeze to death,' Tom said and nodded to Kaisa to indicate she should push herself off.

This run was the best she'd had yet. The snow was soft and there were only a couple of patches where the ice underneath was exposed, making her skis slip and slide away from her. Kaisa managed to control her movements and keep herself upright. Although she'd increased her speed, she was the last of the four to reach the bottom.

'Once more?' Tuuli said to Kaisa when she stopped in front of the three, clearly more competent, skiers. She smiled at her friend and nodded.

This time Kaisa was careful at the top of the lift

and avoided the slippery spot. They took the second of the pistes, running straight down to the men's hotel, where they could have a coffee. Or that was the plan.

It all happened quickly, yet in slow motion. On this slope there was a steep section, which both Tuuli and Ricky took without stopping, making it seem easy as they zigzagged down the hill. As they disappeared from view, Kaisa, who once again was skiing slightly behind the other three, decided to stop on the verge and plan her attack for the rest of the run. She was surprised to see Tom standing waiting for her on the other edge of the piste. Kaisa stopped a little away from him, as competently and stylishly as she could without giving him a snow spray.

'You OK?' Tom said and lifted his goggles onto his helmet, revealing his eyes.

'Sure,' Kaisa said, leaning on her sticks and surveying the slope. She was trying to spot the icy parts so she could avoid them. Her right knee was feeling a little sore. She realised she was quite tired, even though this was just the beginning of the day.

Tom moved sideways up the piste, lifting his skis up one by one, and came to stand next to Kaisa, so that their knees were touching. She straightened herself up and gazed at Tom's eyes. Their intensity made Kaisa's heart beat faster.

'I just wanted you to know how much I enjoyed last night.' Tom placed his arm around Kaisa's waist.

She didn't know what to say. Her mouth felt dry and her heart was doing somersaults in her chest. She felt out of breath.

And that's when it happened.

Suddenly Kaisa lost control of her right ski, which began moving downhill. She attempted to get her left leg to join with her right, but in the process knocked Tom over into the snow. Suddenly she was careering down the steep hill, with her skies at odd angles. She felt the bindings in her left ski give way, as her body tumbled over, and felt her helmet fly away. She realised she'd forgotten to fasten the straps when she put on the balaclava Tuuli had lent her. As she came down, she felt the back of her head hit the ground with force, while still being dragged downwards. Finally, after what seemed like an age, she stopped at the edge of the piste.

'Ouch,' she said out loud, touching her head. The pain in the back of her skull was a dull ache, but her legs and arms seemed to be OK. She sat up and suddenly felt dizzy. The view ahead of her, of snow and pine trees, and a few colourful shapes became momentarily fuzzy and she closed her eyes again and shook her head to try to remove the images. The movement made her head hurt even more, so she sat still, trying to think what to do next.

Another skier, an older man, stopped smartly next to Kaisa and asked if she was alright. But before Kaisa had time to reply, she saw Tom, with one of her skis, next to her. He knelt down beside her.

'Where does it hurt?'

Kaisa fought back tears. 'The back of my head ...' she slumped into his arms.

Tom turned to the man.

'Can you send for an emergency scooter, please?'

TWENTY

That afternoon, on Boxing Day, Kaisa lay on the sofa, with a blanket placed on top of her legs, a glass of champagne in her hand, watching the snowplough working up and down the Tott piste just outside their apartment. Tuuli, Ricky and Tom were moving around in the kitchen, clattering pots and pans. While Kaisa had gone to the emergency doctor in Åre village, her head strapped in a brace to protect it, Tuuli and Ricky had been to the ICA supermarket in town to get provisions. The plan had been to go out to eat that evening, so they had no food left in the apartment.

Tom had skied behind the scooter that had taken Kaisa to the doctor's. Apparently, she hadn't broken anything, and the scan of her head didn't show any damage to her skull. But she was told to see her own doctor when she got back to Helsinki.

'Your skiing holiday is over,' the doctor had said. He looked a little younger than Kaisa, perhaps in his forties, with thin, mouse-coloured hair and pale, worried eyes. 'You're a lucky lady,' he said as he gave Kaisa the results of his examination.

'You need to take it really easy for the next 48 hours. Rest as much as you can and make sure you have someone with you at all times. Any blurred vision, severe headaches or vomiting, call an ambulance. When Kaisa, accompanied by the doctor, returned to the waiting room, she saw Tom sitting on a chair, waiting for her.

'OK?' he said and took Kaisa's arm.

'Are you Mr Williams?' The doctor asked.

'Hmm, no, a friend,' Tom said.

'Mr Williams is no longer with us, I'm afraid,' Kaisa said.

'Ah, I'm sorry to hear that. What I need to make sure is that someone is going to be with you 24/7,' the doctor said, glancing from Kaisa to Tom.

'No problem, I will do that,' Tom said and nodded to the doctor.

Tom had ordered a taxi to take them back to Tottbacken. He treated her like a broken porcelain doll who'd been put together with glue. He held onto her as she got out of the cab, put his arm around her when they walked to the door and wouldn't let go even inside the lift. Kaisa smiled at him and leaned into Tom's solid body. Inside the flat, Kaisa slept in her thermal underwear for a whole hour. She was woken up by a knock on the door.

'Food's nearly ready, do you want something to eat?' Tuuli tiptoed into the now darkened room and, when Kaisa opened her eyes, sat on the edge of the bed.

'How are you feeling?'

Kaisa tried to pull herself up, but the headache had returned and she sank back under the covers with a groan.

'I'll bring you some painkillers.'

Slowly, Kaisa had managed to get herself up, wash and change into a pair of trousers and a nice top she'd reserved for Boxing Day evening. They'd planned to go out to an upmarket hamburger place in the village, but all that had to be cancelled after Kaisa's accident.

When Tom had brought her the champagne flute, she'd said, 'I wonder if I should with the painkillers?'

'Nah, it'll be fine.'

Now, sitting and watching her friends set the table and work together to make her Boxing Day special, she felt a little tearful. She swallowed when she saw Tuuli glance in her direction, 'How's our patient doing?'

Kaisa nodded, she didn't trust herself to speak. She looked at her phone: she wanted to phone Rosa, but feared telling her about her mishap.

'I can come home tomorrow, if you want me to!' Rosa said, concerned.

Kaisa looked at her tanned daughter's face on the small screen of her iPhone. She was radiating the sun and the sea that surrounded her. The skin on her neck and arms had a bronzed glow and her eyes seemed even brighter than usual. She wore no make-up and her dark shoulder-length hair was gathered up in a small ponytail at the nape of her neck. She was drinking beer out of a bottle.

'No, I'm fine, look!' Kaisa turned the phone around and Tuuli, Ricky and Tom shouted 'Hello!'

'You've got friends over?' Rosa asked once Kaisa had turned the phone to face her again. She could see questions about Tom hovering on her daughter's lips but Kaisa just smiled, 'Yes, we bumped into old university friends.'

'Less of the 'old'!' Ricky said.

Rosa had met Ricky on several occasions but she'd never seen Tom.

'Right,' Rosa said.

'Honestly, darling, I'm fine. How about you?'

'Man, it's hot here!'

Kaisa laughed. It felt good to talk to her daughter; her head felt better just from seeing Rosa's smiling face and hearing her voice. She told Kaisa about a group of Swedes she'd met at a hostel. She had made friends with one of the girls in particular and was going to join them for a meal in the small town they were staying in in Northern Thailand.

'There's a Scandinavian Bar, can you believe it?' Rosa said, and Kaisa laughed. She told Rosa twice more that there was no reason for her to come home. The doctor had been quite complimentary about Kaisa's fitness; he'd told her that was the reason she'd not broken any bones.

'You're a hero!' Rosa said, 'I'm going to tell everyone here what a fab mum you are!'

'Oh, Rosa, I do miss you. But,' Kaisa moved closer to the screen, 'I *am* fine!'

'OK,' Rosa said. Kaisa could see her eyes dampen and she said, 'Have fun, darling! Oh, and thank you for your present!'

Rosa had left a Christmas gift for Kaisa, a pair of

silver earrings, with strict instructions not to open it until Christmas Day morning. Kaisa, too, had given Rosa a present, a gold knot ring that she'd seen Rosa admire in the jewellery department at Stockmann's in Helsinki.

Rosa lifted her hand up and showed the ring on her index finger of her right hand. 'And I love mine! Thank you so much for the money, too. I'm going to save it for something special.'

Kaisa had put a hundred dollar note inside the parcel. She knew money would be tight halfway through the trip. She smiled, afraid she might cry if she spoke, and gazed at her lovely daughter. She missed hugging her so much.

Somebody in the background shouted something to Rosa and she said she had to go. They agreed to speak again soon.

'I love you,' Kaisa said, but the line was already dead.

'So how are you going to make up to Kaisa for pushing her down the mountain, Tom?' Ricky said as they were eating.

Tom looked sincerely horrified, 'I didn't push her!'

Kaisa touched Tom's arm, 'It's OK, you didn't push me, I just slipped. I shouldn't have been

standing so close to the edge, or so close to your skis.'
Kaisa looked at Ricky, 'And, actually I pushed Tom
over, but he was lucky to fall sideways.'

'I was joking, people!' Ricky said.

'So how did it happen exactly?' Tuuli said,
leaning over the table towards Kaisa and Tom.

'I just lost my balance, that's all. To tell you the
truth it's all a bit of a blur now.'

Tom nodded, and brushed a few strands of his
floppy fringe back. 'One minute she was there and
the next I saw her tumbling down the hill!' He took a
sip of white wine and began cutting a piece of fish on
his plate.

'Well, I feel bad about leaving you up there on
your own,' Tuuli said and reached out her arm to
touch Kaisa's hand.

'Don't be, what could you have done?'

Tuuli shrugged her shoulders. She was wearing a
navy blouse with a bow at the neck. The colour
suited her and made her eyes glow. She gazed at
Kaisa for a moment, then said, 'I thought I could trust
Tom to look after you.'

TWENTY-ONE

Kaisa spent the rest of the holiday shooing Tuuli out of the door. She was determined her friend would not miss out on the skiing, or the nightlife, because of her silly accident. Even though Tom was with her the whole time, Tuuli was worried about leaving Kaisa, and only spent two or three hours each day outside, hurrying back to Kaisa well before the lifts closed.

The day after Boxing Day, when Kaisa had assured Tuuli she'd be happy to spend the evening watching a Swedish crime drama on TV with Tom, her friend was shocked.

'I can't leave you alone!' Tuuli exclaimed, her face a picture of concern.

'I'm fine! And I'm not alone. Besides, you know I would be happy to just watch the snowplough all evening!' There had been another huge snowfall that day, and Tuuli said it had been difficult to see anything on the pistes.

Besides, what she was saying was true; she was glad of the quiet time with Tom when all the pressure of their newly formed relationship (if that was what it was) wasn't under the scrutiny of their two friends. Kaisa knew Tuuli and Ricky wished them well, but it put pressure on her and Tom. As she lay on the sofa, with time to think, she realised she was falling for Tom. She wanted the relationship to be more than just a holiday romance.

Tuuli crossed her arms over her chest.

Kaisa sighed. 'Please, I'll be in bed by nine-thirty, so you'll just get bored here with us.'

'Hmm,' Tuuli said.

'I bet Ricky has booked somewhere to eat tonight for all of us?' Tom interjected, giving Tuuli a knowing look.

Ricky and Tuuli could plan a revolution together; their organisational skills were visible in both of their orderly homes, with tidy cupboards and not a magazine or newspaper out of place. All of the holidays Kaisa had taken with Tuuli had been arranged by her friend; she knew the best way to find cheap flights, she found the best hotels to stay in and she researched destinations well in advance, booking the restaurants and sightseeing trips.

'OK, if you're sure. To be honest, Ricky has already messaged me to ask me what the situation is,' Tuuli said. 'He's so impatient sometimes,' she added. She hugged her friend and said to Tom, 'I leave her in your capable hands.'

'Go!' both Tom and Kaisa said in unison.

Although Kaisa loved spending time with Tom, she didn't want him to feel obliged to stay with her and kept telling him that he, too, could go skiing during the day and join the others for a meal out in the village.

He lifted his dark eyes from the book on Russian history that he was reading, and said, 'No, I'm not letting you out of my sight.'

Kaisa's heart was filled with such warmth towards him at that moment that she could hardly breathe. *Calm down*, she told herself. *Perhaps the bump on the head is making you misjudge the situation.*

But they did have so much in common. They both loved to read. They had the same taste in TV; Kaisa loved any European and, of course, English drama. She had always been in love with Italian films and they both counted *Rocco and His Brothers* by Visconti among their all-time favourites. The passion for Italy was another thing they had in common: during the days they spent in the ski chalet, Kaisa told Tom about how she'd fallen in love with Italian culture and food when she'd worked in the Italian café Terroni's in London. She told him of the one potentially lonely Christmas that had been saved by the Terroni family. Tom listened intently to her, always close, always touching her with his hand over her palm when they sat at the table, or with his arm around her shoulders when they were lying on the sofa, or just having her foot between his legs when they were sitting opposite each other in the living-room.

Tom told Kaisa about his work in Italy, how he'd left Helsinki soon after they'd met in 1985, when he got a job in an investment bank in Milan. He told Kaisa that the whole of his career was in 'boring banking' and now he worked part-time as a consultant. He told her about his grown-up, 'beautiful' sons and how one was working as a photographer while the other had followed his father into finance.

'What made you move back to Helsinki?' Kaisa asked.

Tom was quiet for a moment. They were sitting at the kitchen table, having finished a rather excellent seafood pasta dish Tom had rustled up from the previous day's leftovers. Then he said, looking down at his hands, which now held a cup of coffee, 'After my mother died, I just didn't see the point of staying in Milan any longer. Plus the politics; it's crazy. If the Five Star Movement wins in March, I don't know what will happen to the country.'

He lifted his head and smiled at Kaisa. 'And as I said before, my ex and her family are quite mad. I think I just yearned for a bit of order in my life. Plus the boys are now grown-up and travel a lot anyway, and they've promised to come to Helsinki to see their old dad occasionally.'

Kaisa nodded. She felt she was losing Rosa too. This trip seemed to have made Rosa more eager to carry on travelling, or even move away.

'Do the boys have Finnish passports?' Kaisa asked, thinking about Rosa's situation after Brexit. She was so happy that her daughter held both British and Finnish citizenship, so could go – and live – anywhere in Europe.

'Yes, they do. Both speak Swedish too.'

Tom got up and put his now empty coffee cup in the dishwasher. 'Anyway, you'll meet them both in a few days when they come for New Year in Helsinki.'

Kaisa looked up at Tom. He had his back turned,

so she couldn't see his expression. The comment was made in a normal, natural voice.

He's expecting us to go on after the holiday.

Kaisa was so shocked by this revelation that she couldn't speak.

Tom realised the significance of the silence following his comment. He turned around and said, 'If that's what you'd like?'

Kaisa bit her lip. Of course, she was enjoying being with Tom, and the sex, well it was something she didn't think she could have anymore. But she was so used to her own company. Plus, could she really trust Tom?

'Sure,' she said, looking at her lap.

Tom stood there, leaning on the kitchen top. Kaisa couldn't look at him.

What's the matter with me?

'You finished?' Tom said, indicating the empty coffee cup in front of Kaisa. She noticed there was a chill in his voice.

'Look Tom,' Kaisa began, but Tom whisked the cup away and interrupted her, 'No need to explain. I understand.'

He went to put the cup and saucer in the dishwasher and closed it shut. He stood there, with his hands leaning on the work surface, and his head bent.

'You'll be OK if I go for a quick walk, won't you?' he said. He was smiling at Kaisa but she could tell she'd hurt him, because the smile didn't reach into his eyes, which had grown darker.

'Of course,' Kaisa said.

TWENTY-TWO

After Kaisa heard the door to the apartment close, she sank back against the comfy sofa, under a fake fur throw. She tried to grasp what had happened. Tom was obviously angry with her, but why? Surely he understood that everything was going very fast, that they'd only been reacquainted for a few days, that they'd only made love a handful of times. Three, to be precise. They were still virtual strangers. Strangers with some history. At Hanken, they had hardly spoken to each other; and then in Helsinki later ... well, the least said about that date the better. Although, Kaisa remembered how lovely it had been to bump into Tom at the Fazer Cafe, just after she'd been to see her old bank manger. At the time, she'd been sleeping on her sister's sofa bed for about a month, and had finally decided to get her act together and start applying for jobs. Tom had spotted her in the queue for lunch and had asked her to join him. He'd paid for the meal and the expensive wine he'd insisted on ordering.

Kaisa had even enjoyed the beginning of her evening with him a few days later. Convinced that Peter had moved on and was seeing someone else, Kaisa had agreed to have dinner at Tom's beautiful penthouse apartment in the old part of Helsinki.

Kaisa must have drifted off to sleep because she didn't hear the door go. She woke up to a hand on her shoulder. Startled, she saw a man's face staring at her.

Tom.

Automatically, she lifted her hand to her mouth to check she hadn't been drooling in her sleep.

'Hi.'

The lines around Tom's dark eyes bunched together and his lips were smiling, 'Sleeping beauty.' He was squatting on the floor next to her.

It seemed he'd forgiven Kaisa for her reticence earlier.

Kaisa lifted herself up with her arms, a quiet groan escaping from her mouth as the pain in her head shot up to her temples.

'You OK?' Now his eyes were full of concern, his brows knitted together.

'No, I'm fine.' Kaisa lifted a hand up, her palm open to stop Tom. 'I'm sure I was snoring and drooling!' she said, trying to shake the sleep out of herself.

Tom laughed, and straightened himself up. 'Ouch,' he said with the effort. 'I think I've been overdoing it on the slopes too! There comes an age when you can't move without making a sound.'

They both laughed, but Kaisa had to cut hers short. She inhaled sharply, drawing in her breath, as the pain in her skull once again reminded her of the accident.

'Are you due a painkiller?' Tom asked, his face once again serious.

Kaisa checked the time on her phone. She nodded, and told Tom where to find the medicine. Her tummy, as she watched Tom's towering shape move around in the kitchen, twisted. He was very tall and his shoulders were wide. He was wearing a pair of dark flat-fronted trousers, a checked shirt under a green jumper. Kaisa thought about how he'd held her in his arms the previous night and felt her cheeks burn.

While Tom's back was turned, she quickly tapped her phone and pulled up the camera app to scrutinise her face. She didn't look too bad. The huge amount of sleep she'd had in the last few days had left her eyes clear and not – for once – bloodshot. Her hair, which she'd managed to wash, was a bit messy, but the waves softened her features.

When Tom left, she'd changed into her satin pyjamas that Rosa had bought her from Liberty's a couple of years ago. The pale blue top had a deep v-cut with buttons, which she knew reflected the colour of her eyes, and the bottoms rested attractively on her hips. She knew Rosa had spent a lot on the present, so she kept the set for special holidays only.

Tom came back and handed her the packet of pills and a glass of water. Kaisa put her phone away. While she took her medicine, Tom settled himself on the chair opposite the sofa. He gazed at her face with such tenderness that Kaisa had a sudden urge to be held by him, to ask him to wrap his arms around her. She wanted to lean her head against his shoulder and feel safe. The way she had done with Peter. Instead, she said, 'Did you have a good walk?'

Kaisa looked away from Tom and through the window, where the snowplough had finished its work, leaving a neat stripey pattern running the length of the darkened piste. The lights from their chalet reflected on the snow, creating a glittering surface, as if the piste was covered with tiny sparkling diamonds.

Tom said, 'It was good.'

Kaisa turned around and gazed at Tom's face. His eyes burned into her. Just as she was considering if she should say something about what they'd discussed earlier, she heard the beep of a telephone. Tom took the vibrating object out of his back pocket and looked at the screen. There was a change in his expression, his mouth became a straight line and his eyes darted from Kaisa to the display on the phone. He got up and muttered, 'Sorry, I have to take this.'

'No, *mon amore*, you didn't interrupt anything!' Tom was speaking in a low voice, facing the door of the flat, his head down and the mobile stuck to his right ear. He was leaning against the wall, turned away from Kaisa.

Kaisa hadn't meant to spy, not really. She was on her way to the bathroom, and had only stopped to listen because of Tom's tone.

'I'm here with Ricky, I told you!' Now he raised his voice and Kaisa didn't know what to do. If she proceeded to the bathroom, which was right by the hall, she'd alert Tom to her presence. It was obvious he hadn't heard her approach and wanted to keep the conversation with whoever it was secret from Kaisa.

Who was it? A girlfriend?

Carefully, Kaisa backed up a couple of steps, purposefully thwacked her bare feet on the tiled floor of the hallway and walked the few paces up to the bathroom.

Tom snapped around, the phone still to his ear and his eyes alert on Kaisa.

'Don't worry about me, I'm just going in here.' Kaisa managed to sound normal, calm even. The bathroom led to her bedroom and she had a good mind to stay there, reading on her Kindle, but now she was stuck. Tuuli hadn't even attempted to make the spare bedroom up for Tom, so for the last two nights they'd shared her bed.

She was fuming. What she had heard Tom say, his face and the look in his eyes, and the way he bent away from her, speaking in a low tone so that Kaisa could not hear what he was saying, meant only one thing: he already had a girlfriend. Or a female friend, a *knullkompis,* or a fuck partner, as the Swedes called it.

What a bloody fool she'd been!

Of course Tom would have girlfriends – or women he took to his bed – right, left, and centre. That's what he'd been like at Hanken, so why would he have changed?

TWENTY-FOUR

'*Fuck, fuck, fuck,*' Tom swore under his breath. He was still standing by the door, with his phone in his hand. Why had he taken the bloody call? Because he'd thought, or rather, had worried, that something had happened to her. She was supposed to be spending the holidays with her parents in the English countryside. Where there was no reception. And why had he felt the need to lie to her? He'd made up his mind, so why delay the inevitable?

He was listening to the sounds coming from Kaisa's bedroom. He heard her move about, closing the door to the bathroom. How much of their conversation had she heard?

Tom walked quickly into the kitchen, taking a

beer out of the fridge. He needed to think. What should he do? Come clean to Kaisa?

It was obvious she already had doubts about him, which hearing, and misunderstanding, his words would just exacerbate. When he'd all but finished the bottle, and Kaisa still hadn't reappeared, he wondered what was going on. Had she heard all of his conversation from the living room? He tried to listen to sounds from her bedroom, but the walls and doors were solid in this place. Just as well, he smiled. The other night Kaisa had been quite noisy. He cursed himself again; he really liked her. Tom glanced at his watch. It was ten past nine. He checked his phone and noticed he'd ended the call with Tiffy nearly fifteen minutes ago. Tom finished the beer and placed the empty bottle on the kitchen counter. He listened again, but the apartment was eerily quiet.

Suddenly he had a thought; was she alright?

He knocked on the door, first gently, and then with a little more force.

'Kaisa, are you OK?'

His phone beeped again and he saw it was a message from Ricky to say that Tuuli was going to spend the night with him in his hotel room.

To give you two love-birds a bit more space.

Tom gave a snort. There was fat chance now that he'd gone and spoiled everything with one stupid phone call.

TWENTY-FIVE

There was a knock on the door, but Kaisa ignored it. She was glad she'd locked the door when she'd rushed into the room. She was now lying on top of the bedclothes. She'd been trying to read a novel, but her mind kept drifting back to Christmas Eve, and yesterday, when they'd talked and laughed, and Tom had told her about his ex-wife. She thought about what had happened when they got back to the apartment, about the Jacuzzi, and about their passionate love-making – or rather sex. And then about yesterday, how gentle and caring he'd been with her since the accident. Her head ached, with a dull, pulsating pounding that she'd never experienced before. What had the doctor said again? She should call an ambulance if she got a severe headache. This was bad, but she couldn't call it 'severe'.

This was caused by the man just outside the door.

All of their time together, all the talk about seeing his sons, that must have been to get her into bed. She pulled out the drawer beside her bed and saw the note he'd left about having 'fun' with her.

That should have told you what kind of man he is.

She looked at her legs in the fancy pyjama bottoms. She remembered what Tom had said to her on the slopes and what she had overheard tonight. Was he just an old-fashioned womaniser, is that it? Kaisa imagined the *'Amore Mia'*, his 'Darling', to be a younger woman, a tall blonde who wore high-heeled shoes and dangled a designer handbag on her arm.

God, what a fool she'd been. What would someone like Tom, who'd always had money and was evidently still loaded, see in her? A widow with a small private income and a grown-up daughter living in the suburbs? Kaisa looked down at her round belly and her thick thighs. She knew she wasn't fat, far from it, but her tummy and legs were that of a woman of a certain age, not one in her twenties.

I bet the 'Darling' has a flat stomach and shapely legs.

No, she didn't want to see, or talk to Tom. The

more she thought about it, the more stupid she felt. Their holiday romance was just that to Tom. Why had she been swooning over him again after all these years? She was in her fifties, for goodness sake! No, she'd feign sleep and let him leave the flat. She had nothing to explain to him, she didn't owe him anything, and she didn't want to hear his explanations.

'Kaisa!' The knocking on the door grew louder.

Kaisa took a deep intake of breath. She moved slowly out of bed. She glanced at her face in the bathroom mirror on her way past, and unlocked the door.

Tom stood outside, looking dishevelled. His brows were knitted and his face full of concern. Kaisa's tummy flipped. He was so handsome; even at sixty, he looked fit and solid. She faced him head on and tried not to let her stupid feelings get the better of her.

Tom ran his hand through his hair and said, 'You OK?'

Kaisa moved her eyes away from his searching gaze. 'Yeah, sorry, the medication makes me really drowsy, I must have dropped off again,' she lied and gave a fake yawn, for effect.

When Tom didn't reply, Kaisa lifted her eyes and looked at him.

'The phone call ...' he began, but Kaisa interrupted him by lifting her open hand towards him, marking their separation. She spoke slowly, pronouncing each word clearly, with her expression as ice-cold as she could make it.

'No need to explain.'

Tom opened his mouth again but Kaisa continued, 'Look, I need to rest.' With that, she closed the door and leaned against it. Her heart was beating ten to the dozen, and she was shaking. How could a man, a man she'd only known briefly when she was young, and only got reacquainted with days ago, have such an effect on her? The anger that she felt against Tom, and herself, surged inside her and she wanted to scream. She tried to listen to what was happening on the other side of the door and eventually heard steps on the stone floor of the hallway followed by one of the other doors in the chalet being closed. Kaisa sighed and went back to bed. She fought tears as she lay down.

There's no fool like an old fool.

TWENTY-SIX

Kaisa woke to hear someone speaking to her through the bedroom door. She raised her body up with her arms, trying to remember where she was. It was still dark, with only a faint light streaming in through the small gap between the curtains. Kaisa shook her head, what time was it? Was Tom still outside her door? She'd had a vivid dream about him, and about a young woman. He'd been kissing her on the sofa in the apartment, right under Kaisa's nose. Kaisa shifted her body, and a sharp pain registered in her head. A small sound escaped from her.

'Kaisa, are you alright?'

'Come in Tuuli!' She stretched over and put the bedside lamp on.

Tuuli walked briskly into the room. She was

wearing her 'city clothes', a smart pair of jeans and a navy blue turtleneck sweater underneath a fitted grey and navy checked wool jacket.

Kaisa gazed at her friend, who seated herself at the edge of the bed.

'How are you feeling?'

'Fine, where are you off to?' Tuuli was not going skiing, that was clear. She glanced at the dark window, 'What time is it?'

'It's just gone three o'clock. Sorry to wake you, but I need to get back to Helsinki. My dad's had a fall. He was rushed into hospital last night.' Kaisa saw Tuuli had put some make-up on; still her eyes showed the concern Kaisa knew she must feel. Tuuli fidgeted with a gold ring on her right hand.

'Oh, Tuuli, I'm so sorry to hear that.'

Kaisa knew Tuuli's dad meant the world to her, especially after she'd lost her mother two years previously to an aggressive form of lung cancer. Tuuli placed a hand on Kaisa's arm. 'We're on the first flight out.'

'Oh!' Kaisa began to move, 'How long do I have?'

Tuuli pushed Kaisa gently back against the pillows. 'No, you can stay. We've got a cab coming to take us to the airport and you'll have the car. I know you can't drive it, so I've asked Tom to take you back to the airport. Luckily, he happens to be on the same flight back, so he can drive you and be with you on the flight and the transfer. You know, just in case.'

Kaisa stared at Tuuli. She couldn't find any words.

'Is that OK? I thought you two were getting on so well, it'd be the perfect solution.' Tuuli looked at her friend questioningly.

Kaisa didn't ever want to see Tom again. The images from her dream were whirling around in her head. But Tuuli didn't need to know about what had happened between them. She just needed to be assured that Kaisa was OK.

Kaisa took her friend's hands into hers and said, 'Of course, that's so kind of you. You don't need to worry about me, just go!' Then she added, 'I'm so glad you'll have Ricky with you.'

Tuuli nodded. She was studying her ring again, fighting tears.

'Come here,' Kaisa reached her arms towards her friend and Tuuli leaned in for a hug. 'It'll be OK,' Kaisa said and patted her friend's back.

Tuuli straightened herself up and sighed, 'I hope so.'

'Let me know how your dad is,' Kaisa said, as Tuuli made her way towards the door.

TWENTY-SEVEN

'You fancy my famous *Tagliatelle al Ragu Bolognese* tonight?' Tom was standing in the kitchen wearing a rather smart black apron, fastened with a knot around his narrow hips, over light-coloured chinos. He also wore a polo shirt under a dark-red cashmere jumper. He had a large spoon in one hand, a packet of spaghetti in the other, his arms wide and the spoon and pasta held aloft.

Kaisa had been trying to ignore him all day. She'd stayed in bed for as long as humanly possible, and emerged into the kitchen well past ten. She hadn't even put on any make-up, although she'd changed into a pair of jeans, a T-shirt and a loose pale-blue jumper. The colour suited her complexion and reflected the shade of her eyes, but she told herself that was a coincidence – she didn't care what she looked like in front of him anymore. Besides, it was clear he didn't fancy her, had never done. It was all a game for him, just as it had been at university.

Tom had been reading a newspaper. Kaisa assumed he'd spent the night in the third bedroom.

'Did you sleep well?' Tom had asked, and Kaisa had answered brightly, 'Yes,' even though she hadn't at all. Tuuli had sent her a message early that morning saying they'd arrived and her father was OK, just a bit shaken.

'Good, good,' Tom said. He'd watched her from the living room as she made herself a coffee and some toast. She didn't offer him anything, didn't ask him anything, but returned to her bedroom and read there until midday.

The sun had come out that morning, bright and beautiful, leaking light into Kaisa's bedroom and the whole of the flat. Kaisa had spent the morning watching skiers ascend the piste next to the apartment, wishing she'd not had the stupid accident. She could see herself going up on the T-bar lift and making her way down slowly, stopping for a coffee or hot chocolate in a café on the slopes. The temperature was perfect for downhill too, only -4C.

It was past one when Tom turned up at her bedroom door.

'Hello, beautiful patient,' he'd said and grinned.

He'd bent over to kiss her cheek, but she'd turned her face away and asked, 'You not going skiing?'

Tom had straightened himself up and shaken his head. He'd run his fingers through the dark brown strands of hair.

'No, I didn't want to leave you alone.'

Kaisa gazed up at him.

'Please don't think you need to look after me. The critical 48 hours have passed. I'm fine.'

Although, she really wasn't. Her head was still sore where she'd hit it on the hard, icy slope and she was still taking the maximum number of painkillers.

'You sure about that?'

The skin around his eyes had gathered into wrinkles, as he tried another smile on Kaisa.

Did he find the conversation amusing? Oh, the man was so bloody infuriating!

'There's no need for you to be here,' she'd said, trying to get herself a little more upright on the bed.

'Besides, look at the weather! You should be up there on the mountain.'

Kaisa had tried to sound normal. She certainly didn't want to play the jilted lover, or the moody girlfriend. She reminded herself that this was just a friendship, which had accidentally (again) ended up with the two of them in bed together.

Why had she let this happen?

'Well, I'm not going anywhere,' Tom said, eyes firmly on Kaisa. 'And, I'm on the same flight as you the day after tomorrow, which is a bit of good luck.' Tom's face had been open, his expression kind.

Kaisa had just shrugged her shoulders and carried on reading her book. Or tried to. She couldn't help but listen to Tom's movements as he did something in the spare bedroom. He'd left the door open to Kaisa's bedroom, but she thought it would be too petty to shut it. She could hear his every step. She listened to drawers being pulled and shut, and cupboard doors slamming. What was he doing?

'I'm going shopping. I should be back in half an hour or so.' Tom had appeared at the door, dressed in his ski jacket and snow boots.

Kaisa nodded, averting her eyes from the smile on his lips.

Taking advantage of Tom's absence, and because she thought it childish to remain in her room all day, she went into the living room and settled herself onto the sofa.

Soon after, Tom appeared in the kitchen, carrying two large paper bags of food, which he began unpacking.

Kaisa glanced at the tall, angular shape, and suddenly she heard something. Whistling? The man was humming, happily carrying a tune. What was it? 'Uptown Girl?' Oh, for God's sake!

'Would you mind putting the radio on, please?' Kaisa said.

That stopped the singing. Tom stepped into the living room, gave Kaisa a sideways glance, and set the radio on a music station. He returned to the kitchen and asked Kaisa about the food.

Had he forgotten that this was exactly the same dish he'd cooked for her over thirty years ago when they'd had a date in Helsinki?

'For old times' sake,' Tom said and grinned.

TWENTY-EIGHT

There was something about Kaisa that was getting under Tom's skin.

Again.

And yet, he had a beautiful thirty-something waiting for him in Helsinki, pining for his company. Tiffy was everything he needed; she came from a Swedish-speaking family, her dad was a property developer, making money from real estate he owned all over the world. Tiffy had studied at Hanken, like himself, and was working for her dad, looking after their portfolio in Finland. She was smart, stylish and liked sex. They'd met two months ago in a bar in Stockholm, where Tiffy had been living at the time. She'd moved to Helsinki only a few weeks later, and now was constantly staying over at Tom's place. Although he liked her, liked her long, slim legs wrapped around his back, liked her sense of humour, there was something about her that made him want to put off seeing her. He didn't know what it was, but often when they were sitting on the sofa, when she'd once again engineered an overnight stay at his flat, watching some Swedish detective series (she adored all the Nordic Noir stuff that left Tom, to put it aptly, cold), he'd find himself drifting off. Tiffy would become agitated, and often storm out of the room. But not out of his flat. To keep the peace, Tom had to go after her and swear that he wasn't going off her. Then they'd have sex and she'd be back to her normal, level-headed self.

All women were difficult in his experience, so it wasn't that. Just look at Kaisa tonight. She'd thawed out a bit, after his charm offensive today. He knew she'd overheard his conversation with Tiffy and guessed he had another woman. But now, as Tom glanced at her, half lying on the sofa, with her legs stretched out in front of her, reading something on her Kindle, she had a smile playing on her lips, even though he knew she was pissed off with him.

Quite rightly.

Tom knew that before he'd begun what could only be classed as a relationship with Kaisa, he should have mentioned that he was seeing another woman, but been clear that it was over. He did feel guilty about that.

Tom had decided to end it with Tiffy before coming on this holiday. More and more, it seemed they didn't want the same things. Like children. She'd let it slip, one evening when they were again on the sofa, watching some Danish trite called *The Bornholm Mysteries*, that she'd like to have a family. The story centred on an abandoned baby, and Tiffy, cooing over the cuteness of the infant, had snuggled up to Tom and said, 'Wouldn't it be lovely to have one of those?'

Tom had looked at Tiffy in horror and said, 'A baby isn't like a new handbag or a fresh pair of shoes!'

'I know, silly,' Tiffy had said and giggled.

He'd suddenly felt like her father rather than her lover. The rest of the evening Tom had felt uncomfortable. He'd feigned tiredness and had gone to bed before the female sleuth (who kept putting herself and the pretty baby's life in danger out of sheer stupidity) had solved the crime. They just weren't right for each other, and he really didn't want to start having children again. He'd done all the sleepless nights, nappy changes and school pick-ups he was going to do in his life. It was unfair to keep hold of a woman who wanted a family, he reasoned, so really, he was doing Tiffany a favour by letting her find a younger man who'd be into all that.

Of course, the stumbling block was that he hadn't technically broken up with Tiffy yet. He glanced into the living room again and saw Kaisa engrossed in her book. He took his mobile out and shouted, 'I'm just going to go and take the rubbish out.'

TWENTY-NINE

Tom had set the table with red place mats and scattered tea lights across the centre. He'd mixed the *ragu* with long strands of pasta, and shaved some Parmesan over the top. He'd prepared a salad of lettuce, cucumber and green peppers, and even made a creamy dressing to go with it. There were cloth napkins, wine glasses and tumblers for water.

'You work as a waiter in your youth?' Kaisa asked Tom before remembering she was supposed to be angry with him.

Tom smiled, shaking his head. His eyes bored into Kaisa. 'I was a "Rich Boy", remember?'

Kaisa sat down and Tom settled down opposite. She looked at her hands.

'Did you ever get your degree?' Kaisa asked.

There were several Hanken students who left the university without sitting their finals. Many employers, especially those with Swedish-speaking owners or management, would pick up students in their final year. With a job, it was more difficult to find the motivation to finish your studies, and in those days no one seemed to mind. Kaisa had learned, however, that those who had not graduated never liked to admit it. Or talk about it. But she didn't care if her question upset Tom. It served him right to feel a bit uncomfortable. And now she saw she'd been right because Tom's face fell and his eyes became serious. He sucked in his cheeks and said, 'Did you?'

Yes, she'd hit the target. Kaisa lifted her chin up and quickly, too quickly, replied, 'Of course I did!'

'I thought that with you going off to marry your Englishman, you might not have had time to take all your exams.'

'What are you saying? That I'm lying?' Kaisa didn't let her gaze leave Tom, who shifted in his seat, and began rolling tagliatelle around his fork. He gave a short, sarcastic laugh.

'No, of course not. Well done, you,' he said and started eating.

There was a silence.

Kaisa gathered a few strands of the long, glossy strips of the tagliatelle. She realised it was very good.

The pasta was perfectly *al dente*, and the *ragu* was meaty, creamy and rich.

Kaisa looked at Tom on the other side of the table after she'd swallowed the pasta and said, 'This is delicious.'

Tom lifted his head and gave Kaisa a quick smile, 'Thank you.'

Again neither spoke for a moment as they rolled the pasta around their forks.

Kaisa was feeling guilty. She was being horrible to Tom while he was quite clearly trying to make amends. After all, he didn't need to cook for her, or stay in the chalet with her. True, her fall, and the incapacity that followed, had something to do with him kissing her on the slopes – if that was what he'd tried to do. Kaisa still wasn't quite sure what had happened. And then Kaisa remembered his voice on the phone call she'd overheard. He'd called the person at the other end of the line '*Amore Mia*'. He'd called her, Kaisa, 'Darling' in Italian before kissing her in the hot tub. And he'd whispered it to her again when she'd sat on top of him and began moving her hips. And the following night, she'd also been his *Amore Mia*.

How many lovers did he have?

Kaisa decided to take the bull by the horns.

'Tom, what exactly are we doing here?'

Tom looked at her in surprise. He nervously brushed the hair off his forehead.

'Having a nice meal?' he said, raising the tone of his voice and lifting one side of his mouth into a grin.

Kaisa sighed, but couldn't help cracking a smile too.

She gazed at Tom and realised she really liked this man.

He was good-looking, of course, and exciting (perhaps *too* exciting!), but at the same time he was familiar. He was too old to want any children (she hoped), and she believed they had similar tastes. And the sex was good. You couldn't get away from how good it was. But, and this was the huge but, was Tom reliable?

Could she ever trust him?

As she ate her pasta, Kaisa asked herself what she wanted. She certainly didn't want a new father for Rosa, she didn't want a husband, but she wanted company. A *knullkompis*, a sex buddy. But more than that: she wanted someone she could laugh with, go out to eat with, to cook for, or who would cook for her, to go to the cinema with, to talk about books with, to have a relationship with, to share her bed with. There it was again: sex.

Oh, my, Kaisa sighed.

'What's the matter?' Tom reached his hand out

and placed it over Kaisa's. His touch was electric. She gazed at the hand covering hers for what seemed like an age. She noticed that Tom's fingers were long and there were a few dark strands of hair growing on the top of his hands.

'Kaisa ...' Tom said. Kaisa could feel his eyes on her but she didn't dare look up. 'I'm sorry,' he added.

Now Kaisa lifted her eyes and saw that Tom's expression was genuinely sad.

Ah, this is it.

She lowered her face and continued to look at Tom's hand on top of hers.

'That's fine, no worries, we had fun,' Kaisa said, the words spilling out of her. 'It's really kind of you to look after me like this, you really didn't need to go to so much trouble.'

Kaisa tried to pull her hand free, but Tom's grip tightened around her fingers. She glanced at Tom's face. His eyes were dark, darker than before. His expression was full of emotion.

'Look, I really like being with you.'

Kaisa's heart was beating so hard she thought Tom might hear it, or see the rise and fall of her chest. She couldn't speak, or look at him, but she nodded.

Tom got up and came to sit on a chair next to her.

He took her hands in his and bent his head to look at Kaisa.

'Look at me, let me see your beautiful eyes.'

Slowly, Kaisa moved her head until her eyes were level with his. She looked at the wrinkles around his eyes and mouth. We are both older, she thought.

'I'm too old to play games,' she said.

Tom's face brightened and he smiled.

'So am I.'

Kaisa didn't respond to his smile, but forced her lips down and looked serious.

'You are seeing somebody, aren't you?'

Tom sighed and moved away from Kaisa, dropping her hands. 'Yes, I was. But it's over now.'

Kaisa considered Tom's words for a moment, watching his face for signs of insincerity. She so desperately wanted to believe him, but could she trust him?

'Look Kaisa, you know I'm no saint.'

Kaisa made a sound, almost a snort.

Tom gave her a glance, but continued, 'I really like you and I would like to spend more time with you.' He moved closer to Kaisa again and lifted her chin with his fingers. He looked into her eyes and said, 'You are beautiful, did you know that?'

Kaisa couldn't resist him. Her eyes melted into his and she let him kiss her. She leaned back on her chair while Tom pushed himself closer. Her whole body responded to Tom, but as she moved her head the pain that hit her was so sharp, she had to let go.

'You OK?'

Kaisa held her head.

'I think I'm due another pain killer.'

She cursed the accident as she watched Tom get up and fetch the tablets from kitchen counter. Her inability to move easily made her feel old and helpless. She smiled at Tom as he offered her a glass of water and a white pill. She took a gulp and swallowed the medicine.

Kaisa rubbed her temples. 'I feel so stupid,' she admitted.

'Why?'

'It was such a silly accident.'

Tom ran his fingers through his hair, 'Look, it should be me who feels stupid; it was all my fault. But I wanted to kiss you so badly ...'

'Oh, Tom.'

Tom lifted Kaisa's hand to his lips and kissed her palm. With his eyes boring into Kaisa, he said, 'Now, how could I possibly repay all the hurt I've caused you?'

Kaisa smiled and touched the unruly strands of hair on Tom's forehead. She brushed it away from his face and smiled. 'I'm sure you'll think of something.'

'I'll take care of you,' Tom said and put his arm around her shoulders.

Kaisa felt safe in Tom's half embrace and dropped her chin against his wide chest. She took in his manly scent and closed her eyes. Tom squeezed Kaisa harder and kissed the top of her head. He then put his lips onto her mouth. Kaisa didn't want the kiss to end; she wanted to melt into Tom, to feel his touch on her body again. His hands moved onto her back, and Kaisa realised he'd unclasped her bra. She sighed when Tom's fingers touched her right nipple. She moved away from him and gasped for air.

'I have to have you,' he whispered and lifted Kaisa effortlessly from the chair and took her into the bedroom.

THIRTY

Afterwards they lay on Kaisa's bed and watched as the sun began to set against the line of snow-capped mountains above Lake Åre. Kaisa was on her back, and Tom was on his side, with his arm supporting his head. He was running a finger down the length of Kaisa's naked body.

'You're very fit, do you know that?' he said and grinned.

Kaisa laughed. What Tom said echoed what the masseur had told her. It was so old-fashioned, and sexist, yet still very flattering.

'You sound like some old Lothario,' she said.

'Less of the "old"!' Tom said and moved so that he could kiss Kaisa's lips.

Kaisa told Tom about the massage and he

laughed. 'I didn't know I had competition!' he said. 'You'd better tell me where to find this Niklas and I'll punch his lights out.'

Kaisa pushed her elbow into Tom's side, 'You'll do no such thing. You never know, it might be what women expect these days.'

Tom shook his head and they both laughed again. 'But he was right, your body is incredible.'

'I must say, I'm pretty impressed with your acrobatic skills in bed too. It can't have been easy with a woman who's nearly concussed,' Kaisa said.

He grinned, 'I think you might enjoy being tied up.'

Kaisa shook her head, carefully, pulling her lips into a pout, 'Sex games already? I hardly know you, Sir.'

'We can fix that,' Tom replied and began kissing Kaisa again. He moved his hand over her breasts, caressing their contours, and then moved down to her tummy and the mound between her legs.

Kaisa sighed with pleasure.

THIRTY-ONE

The next morning, Kaisa woke to a strip of strong light glaring into her eyes from the gap between the curtains. She moved her head slowly, but felt no pain, just soreness in the back of her head. She looked around the bed and remembered last night. But where was Tom? There was no note this time, but had he disappeared once again?

Kaisa opened the door of the bedroom and heard noises in the kitchen.

'Coffee?' Tom asked. He was sitting by the table, grinning at Kaisa.

She nodded and sat down next to him.

'Can we talk?' she said to his back while he was busy with the Nespresso machine.

Tom turned around abruptly and looked at her.

He was wearing one of the long dark blue dressing gowns, revealing a pair of strong hairy legs. Kaisa wanted to go over and undo the belt and push herself against him. She imagined his naked torso underneath and felt faint with sudden desire. She shook her head and looked away from Tom. She needed to keep her composure; she needed to talk to Tom about the other woman. He'd said it was over, but Kaisa realised she needed to know more if she was ever to trust him.

'What do you want to talk about?' Tom asked, placing the steaming cup of coffee in front of Kaisa. As he sat down, the dressing gown opened and revealed the muscles of his thighs. Again, Kaisa had to look away to preserve her equilibrium.

But Tom had seen her eye wandering towards his crotch.

'Let me have breakfast first,' he grinned, pulling the dressing gown down to show a little less. But the fabric flapped open again as he moved.

Kaisa forced her eyes upwards to Tom's face.

'Look, I need to know more about this woman.'

'Ah,' Tom said and leaned back in his chair.

Kaisa looked at Tom's face, keeping eye contact and trying to fight the desire to gaze at his lips. She wanted to lean over and kiss him, and forget all about other women or Tom's proven unreliability. But she also wanted more from this relationship. When she'd woken up alone, fearing what Tom might be up to, she realised that he meant a lot more to her than she'd first thought. It was much more than the sex or companionship. This was the first time in twenty years that she felt she could fall in love. Fall in love with someone who wasn't Peter.

'I think I'm falling in love with you,' Tom said as if he'd read Kaisa's mind.

She must be strong, she told herself. All the same, she couldn't help but smile, and she placed her hand on Tom's cheek.

'Are you sure?'

Tom nodded and kissed the palm of Kaisa's hand.

'But this woman. This *"Cara Mia"*?'

Tom sighed. He turned away from Kaisa and went to stand by the kitchen counter again.

THIRTY-TWO

Tom couldn't look at Kaisa. He already saw in her eyes what she thought of him and he felt ashamed. He knew he should have told Kaisa about Tiffy before they went to bed on Christmas Eve, but he hadn't wanted to break the mood. They'd both been a bit tipsy and it had felt so right to take Kaisa into his arms in the Jacuzzi. And after that he just couldn't stop. Besides, Kaisa had been keen too, almost dragging him to her bedroom. He'd been the one to act responsibly afterwards, tidying up, putting the cover on the hot tub, and washing up the champagne glasses.

At the same time as Tom wanted to flee and not think about Tiffy, let alone speak about her to Kaisa, he wanted to stay and explain how little the woman meant to him, and how much he wanted Kaisa. He'd not felt like this about a woman for a long time; he couldn't remember feeling like this about anyone ever. He realised now that he'd always loved her, from the first time he'd set eyes on her. The way she'd languidly moved, carrying her books over her chest, her long legs and her beautiful derriere in tight jeans. That look, the direct gaze of her blue eyes, made him feel as if she was boring straight into his soul, seeing him as he truly was.

Not what he pretended to be.

Those days at Hanken, he'd not understood that her look was unique, that she was a one-off. And then she'd turned him down; hadn't accepted his invitation to go to the Student Union disco with him. His pride had been hurt; girls didn't usually say no to him. And this girl said no in front of all his mates, so it bruised his young male ego even more.

And then he'd had a glorious, fortuitous meeting with her years later, which he'd completely blown too. To this day he didn't understand what had happened. He'd never failed to get it up before that evening and it hadn't happened to him since. All he could think was that he was so nervous about not missing the opportunity to have Kaisa to himself that his body shut down.

And now here he was, with a third chance decades later, and he was losing her all over again.

This was their last full day together.

Tom turned around and went to sit next to Kaisa. He looked into her eyes.

'I'll tell you all about her, but I have to tell you something else first.'

'OK,' Kaisa said and nodded.

Don't miss this, your last, opportunity.

Kaisa's eyes were even bluer this morning, and her lips looked so soft and inviting that Tom had to exercise all his self-control not to kiss her instead.

'I think I've loved you from the very first moment we met.'

Kaisa started to say something, but Tom placed his finger gently over her lips. 'Shh, I just want you to listen.'

Tom told Kaisa everything. How he'd been too proud to ask her out again, how he'd been aware of her presence and watched her all through the years they'd studied. How he'd thought about her over the years since they'd left university, how he'd considered himself the luckiest man when he'd suddenly seen her in the Fazer Cafe, and how he'd decided there and then that he was going to have her. And how he couldn't explain what had happened during their evening in Helsinki. How he'd looked her up while in London, but finding she was still married to Peter had given up on her.

And, lastly, how he'd wanted to tell her about Tiffy on Christmas Eve.

All through his speech, Kaisa looked at him, scrutinising his face as if she was making up her mind about him.

'Say something,' Tom said after he'd finished and they had been quiet for a moment.

Kaisa smiled. Looking at her hands, she said in a quiet voice, 'You told me to listen and not to say anything.'

'I did, but now I've finished.'

'I can't believe you felt like that about me all those years ago,' Kaisa's voice was still low and Tom saw there was a tear running down her cheek.

Tom wiped the salty drop away from her face with his thumb and took her into his arms.

'Please don't cry.'

Kaisa released herself from him and shook her head.

'I'm not crying, not really. It's just the shock.'

'Oh,' Tom said.

She doesn't feel the same way.

He got up and went to stand by the window overlooking Lake Åre and the houses in the gently sloping valley below. The sun was now high on the horizon. Up in the warm apartment, with the cold snowy scenes outside, it felt to Tom as if they were suspended in a cocoon, away from the outside world and reality. He gazed down at his bathrobe and thought that he needed to get dressed.

He didn't hear Kaisa approach him and was startled when she put her arms around him. Kaisa was standing behind him, pressing her body against his back. Feeling her breasts through the fabric of the thin cotton bathrobe, he turned around and caught her before she lost her balance.

'Careful,' he said and tightened his grip on her waist.

'I think I'm falling in love with you,' Kaisa said, looking up at him. Her blue eyes were liquid and there was a smile hovering on her lips.

Tom kissed and held her close. He noticed she was shivering.

'Let's get back inside the covers. You're cold.' Tom said.

Leaning into each other, they made their way back to the bedroom. Carefully, Kaisa arranged herself on the bed. Tom covered her gently with the duvet and went to lie on the other side of her. He gazed at her face, the gentle curve of her nose and her neck.

She turned towards him and asked, 'When did you and Ricky cook up this blind date of ours?'

'He only told me when we were already here, on the day before Christmas.'

'That's when I found out too,' Kaisa said, smiling. 'I was a bit mad at Tuuli, to be honest.'

'Well, I was embarrassed,' Tom said, before realising that was a lie. 'Well, I think I was afraid, actually. Afraid of my own feelings. And afraid that you'd turn me down again.'

Kaisa lifted her hand and began stroking Tom's face. First she touched his hair, brushing it away from his eyes and then her fingers moved down to his chin, finally touching his lips.

'I think I was afraid too. I think we both knew this Christmas might be a special one for both of us.'

'The best Christmas ever,' he said and leaned over to kiss Kaisa.

THE END

REVIEW THE CHRISTMAS HEART?

If you enjoyed *The Christmas Heart*, please let everyone else know by writing a review.

Thank you very much!

THE ISLAND AFFAIR

CHAPTER ONE

Alicia is standing looking at the vast display of bottles in the ship's tax-free shop when the floor beneath her suddenly shifts and she almost loses her balance. The ferry must be on the open-sea section of the journey. Liam has gone to sit in one of the 'sleeping chairs'. He has taken a seasickness tablet and now feels drowsy. They know from experience that he will be fine as long as he stays still and keeps his eyes on the horizon. Luckily, the quiet compartment has vast windows overlooking the sea.

The ferry travels past the small islands off the coast of Stockholm, before heading for the Åland archipelago. Usually the sea is calm, but if there are high winds the waters are in such turmoil on the open stretch that the crew have to close the bars and restaurants for an hour or so.

Alicia tries to listen to any announcement above the clinking sounds of the bottles, but she can't hear anything. Again, the ship moves abruptly and she loses her balance. She suddenly finds herself looking into a pair of piercingly blue eyes.

She had noticed the absurdly tall man walking along the aisles when she entered the shop. He was difficult to ignore in his trendy jeans, sailor shoes and soft suede jacket. He had an expensive-looking tan, ruffled blond hair and arresting eyes. He's taller than even Liam. But Alicia hadn't spotted him standing next to her until she bumped into him.

He takes hold of her arms. Standing directly in front of her, his gaze is so direct and suggestive that Alicia is flustered.

'Sorry,' she says and the man smiles. The intensely azure eyes, and the slightly open mouth, surrounded by laughter lines, make her own lips lift into a smile. The sensation on her mouth feels strange; she doesn't remember when she has last felt the urge to smile.

Now Alicia feels his strong hands on her elbows. Sensing the heat rise into her neck and up to her face, she looks away, embarrassed.

When did she last blush?

'Don't be, I enjoyed it,' the man says, and his smile grows wider at her discomfort.

She straightens up, and the man's hands fall away from her. For a mad moment, Alicia wishes she could ask him to put them back and hold her, but she dismisses such thoughts and gives a short, nervous laugh.

The man stretches his hand out and says, 'Patrick Hilden.' He has a very Swedish accent, from Stockholm, Alicia thinks. She tastes the name on her lips.

'Alicia O'Connell.' His hand lingers around Alicia's fingers.

'You're not an islander, then?' he says.

'Is it that obvious?' Alicia manages to say. She doesn't know how. She's finding it difficult to speak; she's breathless, as if her lungs have been emptied of air.

'It takes one to know one,' the man continues to smile shamelessly into Alicia's eyes.

'I moved with my mum to Åland when I was a baby, but went away to university and never returned,' Alicia says. She doesn't know why she feels she wants to tell this man her life story.

'Ah, that makes sense. All the best ones leave.' Patrick says.

'And you, you are obviously not from Åland either?'

He laughs, 'Originally from Finland but I now live in Stockholm. One of the unlucky ones.'

Alicia returns the man's laugh. Everybody on the island and in Finland seems to hate the arrogant *Stockholmare*.

After what seems like minutes, Patrick lets go of Alicia's hand but he's still standing so close to her that his scent of expensive leather and something else, a musty, manly tang, envelops her. She knows she ought to take a step back, but she can't move. She looks up at his face and those eyes again.

'You don't sound Finnish,' Alicia says, and then, seeing the man's raised eyebrows, adds, laughing awkwardly, 'Sorry, I didn't mean to be rude.'

The boat shifts again, and Patrick puts his hand out in case Alicia loses her balance.

But this time she's prepared and she steadies herself with a hand on the edge of the drinks display. 'Not much of a sailor, am I?'

Patrick laughs into her eyes. 'You're over for a holiday?'

'Yes.' Alicia replies simply. His scent and presence is intoxicating. She isn't hearing or seeing anything else but this tall, blue-eyed stranger. It's as if he has mesmerised her, and the sounds and smells of the old, sad, disinfectant-scented ship have disappeared.

'Here you are!' Alicia is jolted out of her hypnotised state by an almost equally tall and elegant woman striding towards them, speaking loudly in an Åland accent. When she sees Alicia, she looks her up and down and then, not giving her another glance, turns to Patrick, and says, 'Look, they're about to close the shop. There's a storm apparently, so we need to get a move on. Did you find the champagne?'

'This is Alicia O'Connell,' Patrick says, ignoring her urgent question, and stretching his arm towards Alicia. He turns to her smiling. 'And this very rude woman is my wife, Mia.'

The woman looks at Alicia more closely and exclaims, 'Alicia!' Her voice is shrill and Alicia has a sudden urge to cover her ears with her hands. Instead, she smiles, again. Mia's arms are around her, pulling her into a tight embrace.

'Hello, it's been a long time,' Alicia replies from inside the woman's hug. Her thin, but muscular arms hold Alicia tightly.

'So sorry, I didn't recognise you!' she says, releasing Alicia.

'You know each other?' Patrick says, his eyebrows high.

'We went to school together!' Mia shrieks. 'But we have to get on. Alicia, are you going to be on the island over Midsummer? You must come to our party! Give me your email, will you?'

'Hmm,' Alicia says, not knowing what to say. She

glances over at Patrick, but his face betrays no emotion. He looks more bored than anything else now.

'Oh, don't worry, I've got your mother's address. You must all come. I'll send you the details!'

With that she drags her husband away. Patrick turns and looks at Alicia. With his right hand, he tips an invisible cap on his forehead as if in a salute. Alicia stands there with a stupid smile on her face. She watches Mia speak to Patrick rapidly, like firing a machine gun at him. Patrick's shoulders are wide. She can see his blond hair curl up at the collar of his shirt. She imagines stroking him, running her fingers along his neck and into his thick blond hair.

What's happening to me?

Don't miss Helena Halme's
stunning new novel

THE ISLAND AFFAIR

Out soon

WOULD YOU LIKE TO READ MORE?

'*Wonderfully intimate and honest.*' – Pauliina
Ståhlberg, Director of The Finnish Institute in
London.

Why not sign up for the Readers' Group mailing list and get exclusive, unpublished bonus chapters from *The Nordic Heart* series? You will also get a free copy of the first book in the series, *The Young Heart*, a prequel novella to *The English Heart*.

A standalone read, *The Young Heart* is a prequel to the acclaimed 1980s romance series, *The Nordic Heart*.

The Nordic Heart Series Bonus Chapters

The two bonus chapters are unpublished and exclusive to readers on my mailing list.

The extra chapter for *The English Heart* is from the end of the book, but for *The Faithful Heart* it is from the middle of the novel and takes you to the assignation between Kaisa and Duncan. This part of the story is quite steamy, so be warned.

Get your free book and two bonus chapters today! Go to www.helenahalme.com to find out more.

ACKNOWLEDGMENTS

I'd like to thank David Frise, my first reader, who never misses a wrong phrase, adjective or simile. Thanks must also go to my editor, Dorothy Stannard, for her professionalism and tireless work on this book. I'd also like to thank Mirja Sundström for her friendship and inspiration, as well another best friend, J v R, who provided me with the backdrop to this story. Åre is always in my heart as the most wonderful of places where I can truly relax and enjoy perfect companionship and, of course, the snow.

The Nordic Heart Romance Series:

The Young Heart (Prequel)

The English Heart (Book 1)

The Faithful Heart (Book 2)

The Good Heart (Book 3)

The True Heart (Book 4)

Coffee and Vodka: A Nordic family drama

The Red King in Helsinki: Lies, Spies and Gymnastics

ABOUT THE AUTHOR

Former BBC journalist, bookseller and magazine editor, Helena Halme holds an MSc in Economics and an MA in Creative Writing. Winner of the John Nurminen prize for her thesis on British Politics, Helena is now a full-time author and mentor, and also acts as Nordic Ambassador for The Alliance of Independent Authors.

Helena has published seven Nordic fiction books and one non-fiction title, *Write Your Story: Turn Your Life into Fiction in 10 Easy Steps*. Helena is addicted to Nordic Noir and dances to Abba songs when nobody's watching.

You can read Helena's blog at helenahalme.com, where you can also sign up for her *Readers' Group*.

Find Helena Halme online
www.helenahalme.com